"I would[...] Gary."

Willa paused. "That's what upset me most. My alibi wasn't enough."

Aaron sighed. "We were wrong. I didn't see it for a long time, though. We were trying to find a killer and, on paper, Gary looked like the only suspect. I'm glad Gary was released. And I'm sorry for the hurt I caused you both."

"I wish you'd had the courage to speak up for Gary then."

"I wish that, too, but at the time I didn't see it."

The silence stretched between them. Was she thinking about how he'd pointed out Gary to the sheriff when Olivia disappeared?

"As a law enforcement officer, we have to view everyone connected to a case as a potential suspect," he explained. "Part of our job is to rule people out. Waiting to be ruled out isn't pleasant for anyone involved, but most of the time, the system works."

Are you ever going to forgive me? he wanted to ask, but he wouldn't beg.

WILDERNESS SEARCH

CINDI MYERS

INTRIGUE

For Lucy

Harlequin®
INTRIGUE™

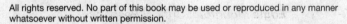

ISBN-13: 978-1-335-69012-8

Wilderness Search

 Harlequin Enterprises ULC
22 Adelaide St. West, 41st Floor
Toronto, Ontario M5H 4E3, Canada
www.Harlequin.com

Printed in Lithuania

Recycling programs
for this product may
not exist in your area.

MIX
Paper | Supporting
responsible forestry
FSC® C021394

Cindi Myers is the author of more than seventy-five novels. When she's not plotting new romance storylines, she enjoys skiing, gardening, cooking, crafting and daydreaming. A lover of small-town life, she lives with her husband and two spoiled dogs in the Colorado mountains.

Books by Cindi Myers

Harlequin Intrigue

Eagle Mountain: Unsolved Mysteries

Canyon Killer
Wilderness Search

Eagle Mountain: Criminal History

Mile High Mystery
Colorado Kidnapping
Twin Jeopardy
Mountain Captive

Eagle Mountain: Critical Response

Deception at Dixon Pass
Pursuit at Panther Point
Killer on Kestrel Trail
Secrets of Silverpeak Mine

Eagle Mountain Search and Rescue

Eagle Mountain Cliffhanger
Canyon Kidnapping
Mountain Terror
Close Call in Colorado

Visit the Author Profile page at Harlequin.com.

CAST OF CHARACTERS

Willa Ryan—New to Eagle Mountain, Willa, a nurse, is Eagle Mountain Search and Rescue's newest recruit. She's attracted attention due to her beauty and her refusal to go out with any of the many men who ask her.

Gary Ryan—Willa's younger brother is rebuilding his life after being falsely accused in the murder of a young girl.

Aaron Ames—Willa's former lover played a role in arresting Gary and is trying to make his own fresh start in Eagle Mountain, but he's never forgotten the woman he loved.

Olivia Pryor—The twelve-year-old was sent to summer camp to get her away from an older boyfriend. Now she's disappeared—was it foul play, or did she run away?

Trevor Lawson—The part-time employee at Kingdom Mountain Kids Camp drove his car into a canyon the night before Olivia's disappearance. Are the tragedies connected?

Scott Sprague—The camp owner is distraught over Olivia's disappearance and spends all his free time searching for her.

Chapter One

Deputy Aaron Ames stood on the edge of the Colorado state highway and stared into the canyon below, his chest tight with dread. A small white sedan was wedged, nose first, between boulders at the bottom of the canyon. A passing motorist had spotted the glint of sun off the taillights and called to report the accident. Aaron squinted, trying to detect any movement in the car. Surely no one could survive a plunge like that. The canyon had to be at least two hundred feet deep at this point.

"Search and rescue are on the way." Jake Gwynn joined Aaron. The young deputy was close to Aaron's age—thirty—with dark curly hair and the deep tan of an outdoorsman. "The highway department is sending a team to block off this lane. We'll help with traffic control."

Aaron turned his back to the canyon and studied the roadway. This time of morning on a Sunday, there wasn't much traffic. Two lanes of pavement wound between rocky spires, sun glinting off the red granite peaks. This stretch of the highway was fairly straight, without the hairpin curves in other sections. "We haven't had any rain lately," he said. "I wonder what sent the driver off the side?"

"No skid marks," Jake pointed out. "I don't see any signs of another driver or an animal or anything." He glanced back into the canyon. "Unfortunately, some people choose to end things this way."

Aaron grimaced, but any reply he might have made was cut off by a siren. Seconds later, a large orange Jeep pulled in ahead of his sheriff's department SUV. The siren's wail still echoed off the canyon walls as half a dozen volunteers piled out of the vehicle and began unloading equipment. His sister, Bethany, waved. His two brothers, twins Carter and Dalton, were also search and rescue volunteers, but they must have been working when this call came in. Sundays were a busy time for the family's Jeep tour business.

SAR Captain Danny Irwin, a tall, lanky man in tactical pants and a blue Eagle Mountain Search and Rescue windbreaker, strode toward them. "Hey, Aaron, Jake."

The men shook hands, then looked down into the canyon. "I haven't seen any movement down there," Aaron said.

"Any idea when this happened?" Danny asked.

"No telling," Jake said. "No one's reported anyone missing. It's pure luck a passing motorist saw the wreck."

Danny looked down at the pavement. "No skid marks."

"Yeah," Jake said. "So maybe we've got a suicide."

"We'll get down there and see what we can find." Danny turned back toward the other volunteers.

"Get a plate number for us and we'll call it in," Jake said.

The highway department crew arrived to set up cones to close the lane to traffic, and Aaron went to help. By the time he returned to the accident site, the SAR volunteers had staged on the narrow shoulder. A man and a woman in climbing harnesses and helmets were beginning their descent into the canyon while other volunteers lined the roadside, watching. An aluminum-framed litter waited at the ready.

Aaron started to join the volunteers, then stopped as his gaze fixed on one young woman, petite and slender, hair in a long blond braid down her back. Recognition jolted him—a knowing deep in his gut, more instinct than conscious knowledge.

"Kat?"

He hadn't realized he had spoken out loud until she turned. The same cool blond beauty—pale skin, blue eyes, delicate features that still haunted him. But the look on her face—surprise, followed by such raw hurt—hit him like a kick in the gut. It had always been like that with Kat—the very first time he had seen her he had felt the connection to his core. He had fallen so hard, and the impact when they had parted still hurt.

She quickly masked her own pain with a cold disdain he remembered from their last encounters. But instead of turning her back to him, she moved away from her friends, coming to stand beside him. "Don't call me Kat. My name is Willa Reynolds now." She spoke softly, so that he had to lean toward her to hear, and caught the soft scent of her hair, a sensory memory imprinted on his DNA.

But her words confused him. "You changed your name? Why?"

"I had to." She spoke in a clipped, angry tone. "Gareth changed his, too. He's just Gary now. Gary Reynolds. It makes it harder for the media and other people who want to harass us to find us."

Her words pained him. He knew things had been tough for her, but not that desperate. "I'm sorry you felt you had to do that," he said.

"Are you?" She glared at him and moved away once more.

He wanted to pull her back, to tell her how much he

missed her. How sorry he was for the way things had ended between them. But what could he say? He had done the only thing he could under the circumstances, what he still believed was the right thing. Why couldn't she respect that?

He had so many questions he would probably never know the answers to. What was she doing here in Eagle Mountain, Colorado, anyway? Surely she hadn't known he was here. But it was so unexpected, that they had each moved so far from their hometown and ended up in the same small town.

She returned, not to where she had been standing, but farther away, where another volunteer was doing something with ropes and the litter. She moved in to help him, her back to Aaron. She bent over, and he had a view of her shapely backside. He forced himself to look away, not wanting to be caught ogling her.

Jake soon joined him. "I saw you talking to Willa," Jake said, and nodded toward where Kat and a young man were moving the litter closer to the edge of the canyon.

Aaron would have to get used to thinking of her with her new name. "How long has she been with search and rescue?" he asked.

Bethany or one of his brothers hadn't mentioned that Kat Delaney was with the group. Surely one of them would have recognized her, whatever name she went by now. Maybe not Bethany—she had moved to Eagle Mountain before things got really serious between Kat and Aaron. But surely the twins would have remembered a woman who was so striking.

"She's brand-new," Jake said. "When Hannah went on maternity leave she recruited Willa to fill in for her. I'm pretty sure today is her first call."

Aaron nodded. Jake's wife, Hannah, a paramedic, was expecting their first child.

"The group is always short medical personnel," Jake continued. "Willa is an RN, a new hire at the local clinic."

Aaron and Kat—Willa—had met when he had delivered a prisoner for treatment at the emergency room where she worked in Waterbury, Vermont. Two thousand miles and a lifetime from here.

"I hear she's single."

Aaron turned to see Jake grinning at him.

Aaron shook his head and turned away. Willa was never going to forgive him for arresting her brother for murder. Never mind that all the evidence had pointed to Gareth. In the end, the district attorney hadn't felt they had enough evidence to convict. The case had never gone to trial, and Gareth Delaney and his sister, Kat, had moved away, leaving behind a lot of suspicions and unanswered questions.

Now they were here in Eagle Mountain. Kat was a chapter in Aaron's life he considered closed. But in a town this small, where it was impossible to avoid running into people, they would have to find a way to at least maintain a facade of distant politeness. The prospect left a sour taste, but was it that different from the compromises people made every day for the sake of keeping peace? He had learned to hold back anger at people who broke the law, and to keep his opinions about some things to himself, out of respect for others. He could pretend he didn't care about Kat anymore. What was one more lie in the grand scheme of things?

WILLA TRIED TO concentrate on the knot she needed to tie, but every nerve vibrated with awareness of the man standing behind her. Aaron Ames. Tall, dark and handsome Double A, as his partner on the Waterbury police force had referred to him. The first time he had looked into her eyes and flashed his confident smile she had been lost. What were the odds of seeing him here, two thousand miles away from Vermont, in a town most people had never even heard of? Had he somehow followed her here? Or worse, did he think she had followed him? The idea shook her so badly she dropped one end of the rope.

"Take your time." Caleb Garrison picked up the dropped rope and returned it to her. A boyish-looking man with a mop of unruly blond hair, Caleb was helping train search and rescue rookies like Willa. He had the kind of patience that probably came in handy at his day job, teaching history to college students. "You don't need to rush," he said.

She nodded, and this time tied the knot correctly.

Danny Irwin joined them. "Sheri and Ryan say they're ready for the litter," he said. "Send a body bag down, too."

Willa swallowed a lump in her throat and nodded. As soon as she had seen the crumpled car, so far down below, she had told herself no one could have survived that plunge. Still, they always hoped for survivors.

"Just the one person in the vehicle?" Caleb asked.

"Seems so," Danny said.

Willa stepped back and watched as Caleb and volunteer Carrie Andrews lowered the litter. She was here to give medical assistance, but the driver of the car was beyond that. Suicide—if this was suicide—was always hard, on the families, but on everyone else, too.

In the weeks after nine-year-old Rachel Sherman's death, Willa had been afraid for Gary. He had been so upset not only by the girl's murder, but also by the fact that everyone suspected he had killed her. Willa had never seen him so despairing; she had worried he might take his own life. She had been furious on his behalf, and more afraid than she had allowed herself to admit. And Aaron, the one person she had counted on to help them through this ordeal, had turned out to be involved in Gary's arrest.

At first, she had told herself it was Aaron's job to follow orders given by his superiors. He had been one of the arresting officers, but that didn't mean he wasn't on her side. She had even told herself it was good that Gary had a friend on the inside. But when Aaron had expressed his own doubts about Gary's innocence, Willa had been devastated. Her brother wasn't a murderer. Why couldn't Aaron see that? The memory of that betrayal still tore at her.

There were a lot of employees at the youth camp where Rachel Sherman had been murdered, but the police zeroed in on Gary right away. They said he was known to be friendly with the girls—as if this was something sinister. They had two witnesses who had seen him talking to Rachel shortly before she was last seen. Just talking, but that was enough to make him their only suspect. It wasn't evidence, and the district attorney had seen that, but not before Gary had been held and questioned for several days.

She and Gary had naively thought when the DA declined to press charges that he would be absolved from guilt, but the harassment only intensified—snide letters to the editor and stories in the paper. Emails and phone calls from strangers making accusations. An outcry from Rachel's family to prosecute him.

"Willa?" She turned to see a young woman with dark braids and a tentative smile approaching. "I'm Bethany Ames. We didn't get a chance to meet at the training meeting the other night. Welcome to the group."

Bethany Ames. Aaron's sister. Willa had taken pains to avoid her, and Aaron's two brothers, Carter and Dalton, at the search and rescue training session. She knew she would eventually have to explain herself, but she wasn't ready to deal with that yet.

Bethany had already been living in Colorado when Aaron and Kat were together, but surely she had seen pictures of her brother's girlfriend. But Willa detected no sign of recognition in the younger woman's eyes. Bethany had probably been too wrapped up in her own life to pay attention to Willa – she had suffered a broken engagement before she left town. "It's nice to meet you, Bethany," Willa said. "And thanks. It's good to be part of the group."

"Not a great first call." Bethany looked over Willa's shoulder at the scene in the canyon below. "So sad."

"Yes."

"Anyway, I just wanted to introduce myself. How are you doing?"

"I'm okay," Willa said.

"Good. It can be overwhelming at first." Bethany swept her hand to indicate the array of equipment and personnel. "All this. But you'll catch on really quick and every one of us is here to help you." She tilted her head, considering. "Have we met before? You look so familiar."

Willa shook her head. "No, I don't think so."

Bethany shrugged. "I guess you just have one of those faces." Someone called her name and she took a step back. "I have to go, but let me know if you need anything, or have any questions."

"Thanks," Willa said, but Bethany was already moving away.

The litter had reached the lip of the canyon, and Willa stepped back to allow those managing it to haul it to the top.

"Did you find any identification?" Aaron's voice shook her once more, but he wasn't speaking to her. He moved forward to meet Sheri and Ryan, who were climbing out of the canyon.

Ryan handed over a worn leather wallet. Aaron opened it, then passed the driver's license to Jake.

"Trevor Lawson," Jake said. He looked at the volunteers who had gathered. "Do any of you know him?"

"I know the name." Grace Wilcox stepped forward. "I'm pretty sure he works at Mount Wilson Lodge."

The lines around Jake's eyes tightened. "That's Dwight's place."

"Dwight Prentice?" Aaron asked. "The former deputy?"

"Right. He inherited the lodge from his uncle and he and his wife, Brenda, decided to continue operating it." Jake tucked the wallet in his pocket. "Any sign of other passengers?"

"No," Ryan said. "We took a good look around, but I'm pretty sure he was alone."

Sheri stepped out of her climbing harness. "He was wearing his seat belt and the air bags deployed, but the car is destroyed."

"Does he have family in town?" Aaron asked.

No one knew. "We'll talk to Dwight," Jake said. "Did you find anything else we should know about?"

"We smelled alcohol," Sheri said. "Like he'd been drinking a lot. That could be a factor in the accident."

"We'll ask the coroner to run a tox screen." Jake looked down into the canyon. "We'll have to arrange to get the car out later, line up a wrecker and schedule with the highway department to close the road while we haul up the vehicle."

He and Aaron walked back to the sheriff's department SUV and stood, heads together, talking.

Willa didn't want to look, but she couldn't help it. Aaron's and Jake's khaki uniforms and duty belts stood out in the sea of tactical black and navy worn by the SAR volunteers. Her eyes met Aaron's and she felt again that buzzing acknowledgment of a connection, humming through her body like a low-voltage current.

She looked away, but his expression stuck with her—not hurt or angry, just *intense*. She had appreciated his serious approach to life when they first met but now, after all she had been through with Gary, she needed more light in her life. She had hoped to find that here in Eagle Mountain. She wanted a refuge and a fresh start, not reminders of the past.

Chapter Two

Aaron and Jake stayed to process the accident scene—at least the portion of it on the highway—then made the drive to Mount Wilson Lodge to meet with Dwight Prentice. Aaron had yet to meet the popular former deputy, though he had heard a few stories. And he was aware that the reason he had a job was that Dwight had left an opening on the small force when he decided to leave and run his late uncle's hunting and fishing lodge.

The lodge itself was a soaring A-frame made of massive logs with large windows looking out onto a turquoise lake—the kind of place people pictured when they heard about a retreat in the Colorado mountains. Smaller cabins were scattered like dice around the lodge, and a sign at the entrance advertised the availability of fishing, hunting and boating access.

Dwight Prentice waited on the front porch as Jake parked the SUV. "Civilian life seems to suit you," Jake said as he and Dwight shook hands. "This is Aaron Ames."

"My replacement." Dwight shook Aaron's hand. A tall man with a thick shock of dark hair, dressed in faded jeans and a denim shirt with the sleeves rolled up, he fixed Aaron with the assessing gaze of a law enforcement officer. "Good to meet you. What brings you two here?"

"Can we go inside and talk?" Jake asked.

"Sure." Dwight led the way through a lobby area with soaring ceilings, to a cramped office.

A freckled blonde, her hair caught up in a clip on top of her head, fine lines at the corners of her eyes, looked up from behind the desk. "Hello, Jake." Her gaze darted to Aaron. "Is something wrong?"

"This is my wife, Brenda," Dwight introduced her to Aaron. He leaned against the end of the desk and crossed his arms. "What is this about?"

"Do you know a Trevor Lawson?" Jake asked.

"He's one of my employees," Dwight said. "Is he in some kind of trouble?"

"I'm sorry to tell you he's dead. His car went off Dixon Pass, along that big straightaway on the descent toward town."

"He went off the road?" Dwight uncrossed his arms and leaned forward.

"Into the canyon?" Brenda asked.

Jake glanced at her. "Yes. Maybe last night or early this morning. A passing motorist noticed the wreck and called it in. When was the last time you saw him?"

"Yesterday," Dwight said. "He's off work today. I knew he wasn't at his cabin, but I thought he might be off somewhere with his brother."

"Who's his brother?"

"Wade Lawson. He's a counselor at the youth camp down the road—Mountain Kingdom. What happened to Trevor, exactly? How did he go off the road in that straightaway?"

"There's some indication it might be deliberate," Jake said. "There weren't any skid marks or other indications that he tried to stop. We don't have a toxicology report, but the first responders who brought him up said the car smelled strongly of alcohol."

"That doesn't sound like Trevor," Brenda said.

Dwight nodded. "I never knew him to be much of a drinker."

"How long have you known him?" Aaron asked.

"Not long. He worked for Uncle Dave and I kept him on after Brenda and I took over the place. He's been a good worker."

"Did he seem upset about anything lately?" Jake asked.

"Not at all," Brenda said.

"He seemed fine to me," Dwight agreed. "You might ask Wade. The two of them seemed close."

"We'll talk to his brother," Jake said.

"Tell him to call me anytime," Dwight said. "I'm sure he'll want Trevor's things."

They said goodbye to Brenda, and Dwight walked with them to the parking lot. "Let me know if you find out anything," he said.

"Is there anyone else we should talk to about Trevor?" Jake asked. "A girlfriend? Other family or close friends?"

"I don't know much about his personal life. Maybe Wade will know more. You could ask the camp owner, Scott Sprague. Trevor did odd jobs for him sometimes."

"Thanks."

MOUNTAIN KINGDOM Kids Camp was only two miles from Mount Wilson Lodge. As soon as Jake turned into the long, wooded drive leading up to camp headquarters, Aaron felt thrust back in time. The countryside around his hometown in Vermont had been dotted with similar summer camps, with their open-air pavilions filled with picnic tables, clusters of batten-and-board-sided cabins, scattered canoes along the shores of a small lake, archery targets set in fields and trees festooned with yarn-and-stick creations or braided-leather ornaments crafted by generations of campers who returned summer after summer.

He spotted several groups of children in matching T-shirts near the lake and a few milling around the cabins as he and Jake parked in front of a square wooden building labeled Office.

A harried-looking woman with shoulder-length gray hair looked up as they entered. "Can I help you?" she asked.

"We're looking for Wade Lawson," Jake said.

A deep furrow formed between her sparse eyebrows. "Has Wade done something wrong?"

"No. Can you tell us where to find him?"

"You should talk to Mr. Sprague." She picked up a radio and keyed the button on the side. "Mr. Sprague, there are two sheriff's deputies here. They're looking for Wade."

"Tell them I'll be right up," said a deep voice.

The woman's gaze met theirs. "If you could wait just a minute."

While they waited, Aaron studied the posters tacked to the wall by the door—instructions on how to thoroughly douse a campfire, first aid diagrams and handwritten lost-and-found notices. Found: Red Flashlight on Lanyard. Lost: One Silver Earring with a Green Stone. He paused before a large poster with a long list of Rules for Campers. At the bottom, in bold letters: "Campers in violation of rules will be punished with loss of privileges. Multiple violations will result in a call to your parents." Words to strike fear in the heart of most children, he thought.

The door opened and a stocky man with a graying crew cut stepped in. "I'm Scott Sprague," he said. "I'm the owner of Mountain Kingdom. What seems to be the problem?"

"No problem," Jake said. "Mr. Sprague, we need to talk to Wade Lawson."

"Call me Scott. What's this about?"

"Do you know his brother, Trevor?"

"Sure, I know Trevor. Is he in some kind of trouble?"

"He was killed in an accident on Dixon Pass," Jake said.

Scott blinked. "I'm sorry to hear that."

"Can you tell us where we can find Wade?" Jake asked.

"Sure. I'll take you to him." Scott turned to the woman. "Track down Veronica and ask her to come over to the boat launch and take over from Wade," he said.

Then he opened the door and exited the cabin.

Jake and Aaron hurried to keep up with Scott, who, despite his stocky stature and graying hair, set a brisk pace. He cut through the trees, headed directly for the shoreline and a dock where a group of girls in green T-shirts paddled about in yellow-and-red canoes.

"Wade!" Scott called.

A slight blond man with gold wire-rimmed glasses—Aaron had mistaken him originally for one of the campers—turned to frown at them.

"Come here," Scott called, and motioned with his hand.

Wade glanced toward the girls, then lifted the whistle that hung from a cord around his neck and blew it. "Everybody out of the water," he called.

The girls had noticed the two uniformed deputies, and stared, motionless, some in mid-paddle. Wade blew the whistle a second time. "Out of the water!"

"You heard the man," Scott shouted.

The girls all headed for the dock at once, resulting in a traffic jam it took several minutes to sort out. But at last all the canoes were beached and the girls gathered in a knot on the shore. A young woman with long dark hair loped toward them. "Mrs. Mason said you needed me," she panted as she approached Scott.

"Take over the canoeing instruction from Wade," Scott said.

Wade had joined them, and was giving the two deputies nervous looks. "What's going on?" he asked.

"These two want to talk to you about Trevor," Scott said.

What little color was in the pale young man's face drained away. "Do you know where he is?" he asked. "Is he in some kind of trouble?"

"When was the last time you saw your brother?" Jake asked, his voice gentle.

"Last night. About seven thirty." He glanced at Scott. Aaron thought he looked nervous.

"Thanks for your help, Scott," Jake said. "We'll let you get back to work now."

"I don't have anything pressing," Scott said.

"We'd like to speak with Mr. Lawson alone," Jake said.

Scott's mouth tightened. Aaron wondered if he was going to argue, but after a tense moment, he nodded. "Let me know if you need anything else," he said, and turned away.

No one said anything until the older man was out of sight, then Wade said, "What is this about? Is Trevor okay? I've been trying all day to get hold of him, but he's not answering his phone."

"Let's go over here and sit down." Jake led the way to a picnic table about fifty feet away and sat. Wade sat across from him, hands clasped between his knees.

"I'm afraid your brother was killed in an accident on Dixon Pass," Jake said. "His car went over the side into the canyon."

Wade made a choking sound and looked away. He swallowed, his Adam's apple bobbing up and down. After a long moment, he faced them again. "Are you sure? You're positive it's Trevor?"

"The photo on the driver's license in his wallet confirmed his identity," Jake said.

Wade blinked rapidly, eyes reddening. He swallowed again, struggling for control. "When did this happen?" he asked, his voice a harsh whisper.

"We're not sure. A passing motorist saw the sun glinting off a taillight and called it in this morning."

"He went off the road? What happened?"

"We don't know," Jake said. "When you spoke to your brother last night, was he upset about something?"

"No. I mean, I don't think so." He looked down at his hands. "I didn't actually talk to him before he left. I mean, he didn't say goodbye. He was just here, and then he wasn't."

"Was that unusual? Him not saying goodbye?" Aaron asked.

"Well, yeah. I mean, he never went off like that before. I didn't know what to think."

"When you saw your brother last night, had he been drinking?" Jake asked.

Wade's eyes widened. "No! Alcohol isn't allowed here. Mr. Sprague would have thrown us out on our ears if he caught us with any beer or liquor." He leaned forward. "Are you saying Trevor was drunk? That's why he went off the road?"

"We're waiting on a report from the coroner. Was your brother much of a drinker?"

"No. I mean, he might have a beer or two from time to time, but he didn't make it a habit. And when I did see him last night, he was stone cold sober."

"Tell us about last night," Jake said. "What time did Trevor get here and what did you do?"

Wade sat up straighter. "He got here around six. He finished for the day at Mount Wilson Lodge, where he works full-time, then came up here. We have a bonfire on Saturday nights, by the lake. Trevor helped me get the fire ready. We moved a bunch of picnic tables down by the water and helped Veronica and Tatum—they're other counselors—carry the food down from the mess hall. We do hot dogs and chips and stuff on bonfire night, roast marshmallows, sing songs and stuff."

"Did Trevor often help out on bonfire nights?" Aaron asked.

"Oh yeah. All the time. Mr. Sprague pays him for that and other odd jobs—cleaning cabins, maintenance and stuff. Trevor was saving to buy a new dirt bike, so he picked up as much extra work as he could." His lips trembled and he looked away.

Aaron and Jake waited, letting him compose himself. After a long moment, Jake asked, "Did Trevor seem normal to you—not upset about anything?"

"Nothing. He was joking with a couple of the maintenance staff who were helping with the picnic tables."

"When was the last time you saw him?" Jake asked again. "What was he doing?"

Wade thought a minute. "We had all finished eating and Veronica was playing the guitar and leading the campers in a sing-along. Trevor tossed his paper plate in the trash, then said he was headed to the outhouse. He walked off and that's the last time I saw him."

"What time was that?" Jake asked.

"About seven thirty."

"Where was the outhouse?"

He pointed behind them. "It's past that first group of cabins. There are a couple of composting pit toilets."

"Were you worried when he didn't come back?" Aaron asked.

"One of the girls burned her hand on a flaming marshmallow and I had to take her up to the first aid room. Mrs. Mason checked her out and decided she didn't need to go to the hospital. We bandaged her up and I walked her back down here to her cabin mates. I looked for Trevor, but when I didn't see him, I figured he had got tired of waiting for me and gone home." He frowned. "But usually he stays to help put out the fire and move the picnic tables and stuff. I tried calling him to ask what was up, but he didn't answer his phone. I was annoyed, to tell you the truth." He rubbed the back of his neck. "It doesn't make sense that he would leave here and get drunk. That wasn't like him at all."

"Was Trevor in a relationship with anyone?" Jake asked. "Could he have gotten bad news from a romantic partner, maybe had an upsetting phone call?"

"He wasn't dating anyone."

"What about other family, or close friends?"

"Our parents are in California and last I heard, they're fine. And Trevor didn't really have any close friends. Just me." His voice broke and he looked away again.

"I need to ask you a question that's going to be hard to hear," Jake said. "But do you think your brother would have taken his own life? Had he ever talked about suicide?"

"No!" Wade jumped up. "No way! Are you saying that's what happened? Because it didn't."

"There weren't any skid marks or any indication that the car swerved to avoid anything," Jake said. "And the first responders who retrieved your brother's body said there was a strong smell of alcohol."

"No." Wade shook his head. "Trevor wouldn't do that. I know he wouldn't."

"Is everything all right here?" They turned to see Scott stalking toward them. He had a short stride, but covered ground quickly, arms swinging.

"Mr. Sprague, they're saying Trevor killed himself," Wade said. "You know him. He wouldn't have done that."

Scott put his hand on Wade's shoulder. "Trevor was a good man, no doubt about it," he said. "But we can never really know what another person is thinking, can we?"

"Scott, did you see Trevor when he was here yesterday evening?" Jake asked.

"I saw him working with the others to get the bonfire ready," Scott said. "I may have said hello, but I didn't speak to him."

"Did you get an impression as to his mood?" Aaron asked. "Was there anything unusual about his demeanor?"

"No. But I was busy making sure the bonfire was organized. It takes a lot of preparation to make sure the campers have a good time, but are also safe."

"Can I see my brother?" Wade asked.

"Someone will call you," Jake said. "And Dwight Prentice says to get in touch with him about collecting your brother's belongings."

"I'll help with any arrangements," Scott said. He was still gripping Wade's shoulder. "Why don't you take a couple of days to pull yourself together and do whatever you need to do? And remember, we're all here to help."

Wade nodded. He stared at the ground, looking miserable.

Jake handed Wade a business card. "Call me if you think of anything we should know, or if you have any questions. I'm very sorry for your loss."

Scott led Wade away and Aaron and Jake headed back to the parking lot. "I know people never like to think their loved one committed suicide, but Wade seemed really shocked by the idea his brother might have taken his own life," Aaron said. "And driving into a canyon doesn't seem like the easiest way to go."

"Still, it happens," Jake said. "Maybe the autopsy will tell us something, or they'll find some malfunction on the car when they haul it up."

"Maybe so."

"Not the best way to begin the week." Jake nudged him. "Still, you met Willa. You should ask her out, though I hear she's turned down everyone else who's approached her."

Hearing this didn't make Aaron feel any better. Had he hurt her so badly she couldn't bear to get involved with anyone else? Not that he had jumped back into the dating scene, either. He told himself it was because he'd been busy—with the move, and a new job.

But really, the thought of starting over, with someone who wasn't Kat, made his chest hurt. Now that he knew she was here, the pain had started up again. No sense going out of his way to make it any worse.

Chapter Three

When Willa arrived home from running errands Sunday afternoon, Gary was just coming out of the shower. Neither of them could afford rent on their own, so sharing a place had made the most sense. Plus, it allowed Willa to keep an eye on her little brother. He would have protested that, at twenty-three, he didn't need her to look after him, but she needed to reassure herself that he was all right.

"How was your day?" she asked as she put away groceries.

"Okay." He rubbed his shoulder. "I had to dig, like, a mile of ditch for a water line."

"By yourself? That sounds horrible."

"I was supposed to have help, but the guy didn't show up. And it had to be done today. Supposedly there's a big storm coming in tonight."

"Maybe you should look for another job."

He had a degree in physical education but all he had been able to find here was a job doing maintenance at a local ranch.

"Nah. I like this one. Working outside, nobody to hassle me. And it keeps me in shape." He moved to the refrigerator and took out a can of flavored seltzer. "You want anything?"

"No, thanks." She closed the cabinet, then stood by the counter, unable to think what to do next.

"Is something wrong?" Gary asked.

"What makes you ask that?"

"You look upset." He took a drink of seltzer, gaze fixed on her. "Did something happen at the clinic yesterday?"

"We had a bad search and rescue call this morning. A guy drove his car off Dixon Pass. They think he did it deliberately."

"Wow. That's rough. Was he really messed up?"

"No. I mean, I don't know. I didn't see him."

"Maybe you shouldn't do this search and rescue stuff if it's going to upset you so much."

"It's not the call that upset me."

He frowned. Before he could ask any more questions, she added, "I saw Aaron today. He was at the scene. He's a sheriff's deputy. Here, in Eagle Mountain." There. She had told him. She hated to upset him, but he needed to know. Better to hear the news from her than to run into Aaron somewhere in town.

But Gary didn't look upset. "Yeah, I know."

"You knew?" Her vision grayed at the edges for a moment, she was so shocked. "And you didn't tell me?"

He shrugged. "Because I knew it would upset you. And see, it has." He gestured to her with the seltzer can.

"When did you see him? Did he say anything to you?"

"I was at the hardware store, and I saw him outside, talking to someone. He didn't see me. Then I saw him one other time, at Mo's Pub. We never spoke. It was no big deal. Did he say anything to you?"

"He said he was sorry."

"Maybe he really is."

She hugged her arms across her stomach. "I don't care

if he's sorry or not. I can't forgive him for believing you would ever do something so horrible."

"What did you expect? He's a cop. That's how they're trained to think." He drained the rest of the can of seltzer and tossed it into the recycling bin.

"But there wasn't any evidence against you."

"There wasn't any evidence against anyone else, either. And two people saw me talking to Rachel that night."

"How can you be so calm about something so horrible?"

He had spent time in jail because of police insistence on focusing on him as their only suspect in Rachel Sherman's murder. The two of them had had to leave everything behind and start over because of that terrible mistake.

Gary shrugged. "I don't see any sense in brooding over something that happened in the past that was completely out of my control. I'd rather get on with my life."

It was a sensible attitude. A healthy one. But one she couldn't adopt. "Aaron should have given you the benefit of the doubt," she said.

"I don't think that's how these things ever work. And it's not like he was the only cop pointing the finger at me. He wasn't even a detective or an investigator. The important thing is that the DA didn't file charges and I'm a free man now." He opened the refrigerator again. "Spaghetti sound good for dinner? I'll make it."

"Sure. Thanks."

But he didn't start dinner right away. He continued to study her. "Don't let Aaron get to you," he said. "He made a mistake and he paid for it. He lost you. Someone else will step up to the plate and realize how great you are. In case you haven't noticed, this place is crawling with single men. Seriously, I can't believe you don't have guys standing in line to ask you out."

She laughed, more from frustration than mirth. "I'm not interested in going out with anyone right now." She had turned down half a dozen men who had shown up at the clinic, asking to see "the new nurse" with their mystery ailments. They had all been polite, ranging from slick and charming to bashful and sweet.

"That's cool, too." He pulled a package of ground beef from the refrigerator and shut the door. "But the next time you see Aaron, look right past him. Let him know you don't care what he thinks."

"I'll do that." She didn't need Aaron. She didn't need any man.

But she did need for Gary to be all right. He said he was free now, but was he, really? The two of them had given up so much to escape the cloud that hung over him because of those charges. They had told themselves taking new names and moving was a chance to reinvent themselves. They could do whatever they wanted, and be whoever they wanted to be.

But seeing Aaron had made her feel the past would always be hanging on to their heels, pulling them backward whether she wanted it or not.

THEIR SHIFTS HAD ended by the time Jake and Aaron left Mountain Kingdom Kids Camp, but they still needed to return to the station and file reports. Aaron was used to the long hours. It wasn't as if he had anything else to devote himself to, though he knew Jake was anxious to get home to his wife.

"I wonder why Trevor left the bonfire without speaking to his brother?" Jake asked as he and Aaron drove away from the camp. "And how he ended up smelling of alcohol if he wasn't a drinker?"

"Maybe he wasn't drinking at all. Maybe a bottle broke in the car or something."

"Yeah. We need to wait until we hear from the coroner." He slowed as a quartet of turkeys crossed the road in front of them, sun angling through the trees glinting off their bronzed feathers. "Did you ever go to summer camp as a kid? Someplace like Mountain Kingdom?"

"I spent a couple of weeks at Boy Scout camp one summer," Aaron said. "But not places like this, where kids stay for a month at a time, or the whole summer. There were a lot of those in Vermont, where I'm from. When I was on the force in Waterbury, we would occasionally get calls."

"What kind of calls?"

"Usually petty things—theft or vandalism. But we had a murder case once. A little girl was killed." Rachel Sherman.

"Did they find the killer?"

"We never did."

"That's rough."

"Yeah." Aaron and another officer had interviewed the girls in Rachel's cabin. They had said they had seen Rachel talking to Gareth Delaney. Aaron remembered the shock of hearing Kat's brother's name in connection with a crime. He hadn't known Gareth well, but he had seemed like such an ordinary, likable guy.

But the more Aaron and his fellow officers talked to Gareth, the more nervous and suspicious Gareth acted. At first he denied knowing Rachel. When confronted with her cabin mates' statements, he admitted talking to her, but said he hadn't even known her name. Another lie. And though everyone was supposed to be innocent until proven guilty, you didn't have to be a cop long to learn that guilty people often lied.

Aaron realized Jake had been talking to him. He shook his head. "Sorry. What did you say?"

"I asked how you're settling in. New town, new job, all that?"

"It's good. I like it here."

"Small towns aren't for everyone, but I guess it helps that you have family here."

"Yeah. It's great." Not that he couldn't have moved away from his parents and siblings, but when they had decided to follow his sister, Bethany, to Eagle Mountain, it seemed like a good opportunity for him to make a fresh start. Get away from bad memories.

Except this morning the biggest memory had confronted him on the side of the highway. As beautiful as he remembered.

And just as unforgiving.

WILLA SLEPT little that night, her mind too full of worries about Aaron and Gary. Would Aaron spill their secret to others in the community? Would the media—or some true-crime enthusiast online—track them down and make their lives miserable, as had happened back in Waterbury? The murder of Rachel Sherman remained unsolved and the internet was full of amateur sleuths who were sure they could find the real killer. A good number of those people started with the assumption that Gary was guilty. All they had to do was find the right proof to convict him, or persuade him to confess.

She dozed off after 4:00 a.m. and woke at six to crashing thunder and pounding rain. She gave up trying to sleep and rose, showered and made coffee. By seven, she was sipping her second cup, scrolling through her phone, searching for any distraction, when it vibrated in her hand with an alert from the first responders' app. For a moment she thought she must have dreamed the last hour as she read the message:

Volunteers needed to search for missing girl, Mountain Kingdom Kids Camp. Muster at SAR Headquarters.

She was still staring at the message when Gary shuffled into the kitchen. He must have said something, but she didn't hear him. Her head buzzed with the dizzying sensation of having been here before.

"Sis? Is something wrong? You look like you're going to be sick."

She looked up and focused on her brother's face: He was blond like her, with a boyish face that had many people still mistaking him for a teenager. Despite everything that had happened to him, he maintained his open, optimistic attitude about life. People liked Gary. They trusted him.

Most people did. The cops hadn't. Aaron hadn't.

She wet her dry lips, and struggled to speak. "It's a search and rescue call," she said. "There's a girl missing from a kids camp."

Alarm flashed in his eyes. "What camp?"

"Some place called Mountain Kingdom Kids Camp."

He groped for a chair and sank into it, so pale even the blond hairs of his unshaven chin stood out against his pasty skin. "Who? Did they say who?"

"They don't say." She leaned forward and covered his hand with hers. "What's wrong? Why are you acting like this?"

He wiped his hand across his face, and wouldn't meet her gaze. "Mountain Kingdom is where I work."

He wasn't making any sense. "You work at a ranch."

"That's what I told you, but I actually work at the camp." He grimaced. "I didn't tell you because I knew you'd lose it."

Her stomach clenched. "Gary, how could you do that? How could you risk that?"

"It was the only job I could find, okay? And it's a good one. I didn't have anything to do with Rachel's death, so what does it matter if I work at this camp instead of that one? I didn't do anything wrong."

"Of course you didn't. But what if someone finds out about what happened in Vermont—what you were accused of? They could jump to the wrong conclusion."

They could think he had sought out another job working with kids on purpose. That he was some kind of predator.

"Whatever they think, it's not true. We have to live in the present, sis. Not stay stuck in the past."

She wanted to argue with him that their present was shaped by the past, but her phone buzzed again, reminding her she didn't have time for this. "I have to go," she said, and stood.

"I should go, too," he said. "Maybe I can help."

"No. I don't want you anywhere near the camp or this girl. Not until she's safe. I won't risk anyone thinking you had anything to do with her going missing."

"I didn't."

"I know. But it will be better if you stay away."

He didn't say anything, just stared at her, jaw set in a stubborn line. She turned away, her heart pounding and a voice in her head chanting over and over, *This can't be happening again.*

Chapter Four

As the volunteers assembled to begin the search for thirteen-year-old Olivia Pryor, Willa reminded herself that a
missing child didn't mean she was a victim of foul play.
Children wandered off and got lost all the time. They sometimes ran away. Most of them were found safe. Surely that
would happen this time, too.

"As a reminder for those of you who are new, we're going
to search in teams." Captain Danny Irwin addressed the
assembled volunteers at Eagle Mountain Search and Rescue headquarters. Almost two dozen volunteers had responded to the early-morning summons, despite the rain
that pounded so loudly on the metal roof of the headquarters building that Danny had to raise his voice in order to
be heard.

"Each team of four to five people will search an assigned
area, as indicated on this map." Danny held up a piece of
copy paper. "Anna Trent and her search dog, Jacqui, are
already headed for the camp to see if Jacqui can pick up
Olivia's scent. With a lot of luck, by the time we get there,
they'll have located the girl and we can all go home. But
the rain is going to make things more difficult, so we need
to be prepared to conduct a ground search."

He consulted the piece of paper in his hand once more.

"Olivia is five feet, one inches tall and weighs approximately one hundred pounds. She has sandy brown hair, olive skin and brown eyes. There's a photo of her on the map each of you will be given. She was reported missing this morning when a bunk mate told her counselor that Oliva wasn't in her bunk. Another cabin mate said she thought Olivia had sneaked out of the cabin a little after midnight."

"She's probably hiding somewhere, trying to stay out of this rain," someone in the back of the room said.

"Keep that in mind as you're searching," Danny said. "Also remember that she may believe she's in trouble for sneaking out of the cabin, so she might not respond to your calls, even if she hears you. It's not unusual for children to hide from searchers. There's also the possibility she's hurt and unable to respond, so don't rely solely on your sense of hearing. Search for flashes of color or anything out of the ordinary in your surroundings such as piles of brush or dislodged rocks or broken branches."

"We might find footprints in the mud," someone else said.

"Or the rain might wash them away," someone else countered.

"Do we know what she was wearing when she left?" Bethany Ames, standing a short distance from Willa, asked.

"We don't," Danny said. "Though the usual camp uniform is shorts or jeans and T-shirts."

"Let's hope she thought to put on a raincoat," someone said.

"Any more questions?" Danny asked.

No one had any, so they headed out to the parking lot for the drive to the camp. Willa found herself in an SUV with Bethany, Grace Wilcox, Tony Meisner and Harper Stanick.

There was little conversation on the drive to the camp, the steady thump of windshield wipers and the drum of rain-drops providing background noise for their thoughts. Willa texted Gary with Olivia's name and information, asking if he knew the girl, but he made no reply.

Mountain Kingdom Kids Camp looked like a typical summer retreat, with clusters of wooden cabins, a main lodge and recreation areas set amid tall pine trees. This morning the grounds teemed with people in uniform—both camp staff and law enforcement. A deputy checked them in at the front gate and directed them to a staging area in front of the main lodge, an impressive log-and-glass struc-ture where at least twenty people—all adults, from what Willa could see—milled about in plastic ponchos or more substantial rain gear.

Willa pulled the hood of her rain jacket over her hair as she exited the SUV and looked around. She didn't realize she was searching for Aaron until she spotted him stand-ing with two other deputies at one corner of the lodge. He wore a black raincoat, but the bottoms of his khaki uniform pants were soaked.

She turned away, hoping he wouldn't see her, but as she shifted her gaze another familiar figure made her gasp. Gary was there, talking to another young man. They were both wearing green jackets with an emblem on the chest she assumed was the camp's logo. As if he had heard her he looked up, his expression defiant.

"Thank you all for coming." An older man had mounted the steps leading to the lodge entrance and was address-ing the gathered crowd with a hailer. He, too, wore a green rain jacket and green rain pants. He had pushed back the hood of the jacket to reveal a gray crew cut. He had a beefy build but he wasn't fat. Willa guessed he was in his late forties. "My name is Scott Sprague and my family has owned and managed Mountain Kingdom Kids Camp for forty years," he said. "This is the first time we've had to deal with something like this, and I want to thank you all for coming to help. Olivia is a bright, smart child, and I'm confident she'll be found safely. But she could be hurt, or scared, or just confused. So I want to ask you to be gentle with her when you find her. Don't worry about finding out what happened. We don't care about that. We just want her safely returned to us." He lowered the hailer and looked out at them, the picture of a man in distress.

Willa was paired with Grace, Tony and Bethany to search an area near the camp's kitchen and mess hall. A group of camp employees were combing through the interior of the buildings. Willa's group was supposed to cover the exterior between the buildings and the lake, to a group of campers' cabins on the east and a dirt road on the west. They kept close together, looking behind and up in trees, behind boulders and along the foundations of the buildings. They investigated two pit toilets, a massive rock barbecue grill, and turned over half a dozen canoes beached along the lakeshore, in case Olivia had taken shelter there. All the while the rain beat down. Within ten minutes Willa was shivering and clammy, despite her rain gear.

Her phone buzzed and she answered the call. It was Danny. "Willa, can you return to the headquarters building? We've got one of the campers who slipped and hurt her leg. She might need some medical attention. I'm tied up in another part of the camp."

"Of course. I'll be right there." She ended the call, then told the others what had happened and left them. She spotted other SAR volunteers, law enforcement officers and camp employees searching for Olivia as she hurried toward the lodge. The sound of the girl's name rang out from all directions. Though the rain had slackened a little, water still dripped from trees and the sun remained behind heavy cloud cover, lending the whole scene a twilight feeling.

The girl in question—two thin brown braids framing a round face, with a streak of mud on one cheek—sat on a sofa in the lobby, one foot on a pile of cushions. She looked as if she had been crying. "I was just trying to find my friend," she said before Willa could even ask her name. "I know I wasn't supposed to be out of the cabin, but I couldn't sit in there and do nothing. Am I going to be in trouble?"

A young woman with swimmer's shoulders and short blond hair sat next to the injured girl on the sofa. "I'm Tatum," she said. "And this is Stella. She was climbing on some rocks behind her cabin and slipped and fell."

"Stella, I'm Willa. I'm a nurse. What hurts?"

"My ankle." Stella leaned forward and gingerly touched her left ankle. "It hurts a lot." Tears welled, and clung to her thick lashes.

"I got her shoe off right away," Tatum said. "But I left the sock so maybe her foot wouldn't be so cold."

The foot was ice-cold, to be expected with this damp. "Maybe you could find a couple of blankets," Willa said as she gently examined the swollen foot.

Stella cried out when Willa tried to move the foot, and Willa took her hands away. "No more of that," she said. "But I think you've sprained it. To be sure, you'll need to have an X-ray."

"My parents are going to be so mad," she wailed.

"They'll be relieved you're okay," Willa said.

"You don't know my parents."

"No. But think about it. One girl is missing. They'll hear about that. Then they'll learn that you're hurt, but safe. In comparison, an injured ankle isn't going to seem like a big deal."

"I can't believe all these people are looking and they haven't found Olivia," Stella said.

"I hope they'll find her soon." Willa opened her pack and took out a roll of elastic bandage. "I'm going to wrap your ankle," she said. "That's going to make it feel a lot better. We'll also get an ice pack for you."

Stella sniffed and watched as Willa began to wind the tape around her foot and ankle. "Are you in the same cabin as Olivia?" Willa asked.

"Yeah. She and I are good friends."

"When was the last time you saw her?"

"About ten o'clock. That's lights out. We said good-night."

"I heard she sneaked out of the cabin later."

Stella sighed. "I guess so. She's done it before. I didn't see her this time, but Marissa did, and she wouldn't have any reason to lie."

"Why did Olivia sneak out?" Willa said.

Stella didn't say anything. Willa focused on wrapping the ankle, letting the silence tease an answer from the girl. "I think she was meeting someone," Stella said at last.

"Another girl?" Willa asked. "Or a boy?"

"Probably a boy." She looked up as Tatum returned.

"I found a couple of blankets," Tatum said, and laid them on the sofa next to Stella. "And I brought an ice pack." Her eyes met Willa's, then she turned to Stella. "I heard what you said about Olivia sneaking out." She shrugged, deliberately casual. "It happens. I mean, there are rules, but not everybody follows them. Do you know who she was meeting? One of the other campers?"

"I don't know," Stella said. "Honest, I don't. She wouldn't say." She looked miserable.

Willa gently patted the wrapped ankle. "Does that feel better?" she asked.

"A little."

Willa settled the ice pack in place. "She's going to need X-rays," she told Tatum.

"Mrs. Mason is going to take her to the clinic in town in a little bit," Tatum said. She turned back to Stella. "Did Olivia tell you anything else? Maybe about her boyfriend back home?"

"You know about that?" Stella's eyes widened.

"I heard her parents sent her to camp to get her away from an older boy she had been seeing," Tatum said. She glanced at Willa. "She wouldn't be the first camper to come here in an effort to get her away from someone the parents thought inappropriate."

"Olivia said her boyfriend was sixteen," Stella said. "But that they weren't doing anything wrong."

"It might help find Olivia if the sheriff knew about this," Willa said. "Someone could try to track down this person Olivia had been going to meet."

"Good idea." Tatum pulled a radio from her pocket. "I'll let someone know." She took a few steps away.

"I'm really going to be in trouble now, aren't I?" Stella said.

"You're helping your friend," Willa said. "No need for you to be in trouble for that."

"Will you stay with me until Mrs. Mason gets here?" Stella asked.

"Of course." She was finally beginning to feel warm again, and Stella was a sweet child. She liked Tatum, too, who was close enough to Stella's age—was she even eighteen?—to sympathize with the girl.

Willa regretted that decision when she heard footsteps approaching and turned to see an older woman walking toward her, accompanied by a sheriff's deputy. An expression Willa couldn't read passed across Aaron's handsome face when he recognized her, but he quickly masked it, and focused on the girl.

"Hello, Stella," he said. "I'm Deputy Ames. I understand you have some information that might help us find your friend Olivia."

Stella picked at the pink and purple woven bracelet around her left wrist. "I don't know if it will help or not. I mean, I didn't actually see Olivia leave the cabin."

Aaron sat on the sofa beside the girl, but not too close. "Tell me what you know," he said. "I promise, you're not in trouble. But the more information we have, the better we'll be able to narrow our search and find Olivia."

"All I know is that Olivia had sneaked out of the cabin before. She went to meet someone, but she wouldn't say who."

"Did she have any special friends among the other campers?" Aaron asked. "Boys or girls?"

"No one in particular." She bit her bottom lip, then looked up, as if just realizing something. "I can't think of a single time I ever saw her even talk to a boy. I mean, they're all the time trying to get our attention, or teasing us. But Olivia ignored them all. So it couldn't have been a boy she was meeting." Stella looked relieved.

"What about staff?" Aaron asked. "Was Olivia friendly with any of them?"

"Veronica is our counselor," Stella said. "We're all

friendly with her. And Tatum. She does crafts with us and stuff."

"What about male staff?" Aaron asked. "Did you ever see Olivia talking to one of them?"

Willa stiffened. She thought she knew where this was going and she didn't like it.

Stella shifted, as if suddenly uncomfortable. "The other male counselors—Wade and Crispin—tell us what to do, or they'll ask questions if they're teaching us something. And Mr. Sprague talks to all of us if he sees us. He's always asking how we're doing and stuff like that."

"Did you ever see Olivia alone with any of the staff members?" Aaron asked. "When they weren't instructing you?"

Stella shook her head. "No."

"Tatum said something about Olivia having a boyfriend back home," Aaron said. "Did she ever say anything about him coming to see her here?"

"No." Stella brightened. "Do you think that's what happened? Maybe they ran away together. I mean, if he's sixteen he can drive, right?"

"Did she ever mention running away with this boy?" Aaron asked.

"No."

"What did she tell you about him?" Aaron asked.

Stella slumped, her elation having vanished. "She said after her parents found out she was sneaking off to see him, they made him promise to never contact her again and he hadn't. She was kind of mad about that and said she never wanted to see him again."

"Was Olivia happy here at camp?" Aaron asked.

Stella considered the question. "She seemed to really like it here until a couple of weeks ago."

"What happened a couple of weeks ago?" Aaron asked.

"I don't know. She just…" She ducked her head, gnawing her bottom lip again.

"Just what?" Aaron prompted.

"She was crying one night, after lights out. I asked her what was wrong and she just said she wanted to go home."

"Do you have any idea what was wrong? Do you remember anything happening?"

"I thought she was just homesick. We all feel that way sometimes."

"After that, was she still homesick?"

"She was just…quieter. Like maybe she was sad. But she didn't want to talk about it."

"Anything else you think we should know? Anything that might help us find her?"

"I'm sorry. I can't think of anything."

"Thank you for your help." He stood. Mrs. Mason moved forward. "I've got my car at the front door," she said. "Tatum has a wheelchair."

Tatum wheeled the chair forward and Stella left with her and Mrs. Mason.

When they were alone, Aaron turned to Willa. "I saw your brother. I was surprised to find out he works here."

Willa didn't mention that she had been surprised, too. "He was home with me all night," she said. "Until after I got the search and rescue call that Olivia was missing."

"Are you sure?" Aaron asked. "He could have slipped away while you were asleep."

"And abducted a girl in the middle of the night? I can't believe you're suggesting something so ridiculous." She struggled to keep her voice down, but fury made her shake. She clenched her fists, fighting the urge to physically attack him.

"It's my job to ask hard questions," he said. "Of everyone." Everything about him was hard—his voice, his clenched jaw, the look in his eyes. Cop mode, she had thought of it, before she had to face the demeanor herself after Gary was arrested.

"I've given you my answers," she said. "Why can't you accept them?" She didn't wait for his reply, but turned and stalked across the lobby, aware of the stares of people milling about the space.

"Aaron!"

Another deputy—a muscular blond—entered the lobby. He hurried past Willa and he and Aaron met beneath a massive antler chandelier in the middle of the space. They conferred, heads together, then raced outside, feet pounding hard on the floor, faces taut with urgency.

Willa hurried after them. She found Danny with a group of other people just outside. "What's going on?" she asked, reading the same urgency on his face.

"They've found something," he said. "Something that might be related to Olivia."

Chapter Five

Aaron stood with Deputies Shane Ellis, Jake Gwynn, Jamie Douglas, Ryker Vernon and Sheriff Travis Walker in a tight circle in an L formed by the cabin where Scott Sprague lived and a maintenance shed. Search and rescue volunteer Anna Trent was also there, holding tightly to the leash of a black standard poodle who wore a blue Search Dog vest. They were all staring at a ripped and muddy green T-shirt, splotched with a rusty red Aaron thought looked like blood.

"The dog located it at the corner of the foundation," the sheriff said. "That kept the worst of the rain off of it."

"And we're sure it belongs to Olivia?" Jamie asked. Her long hair had partially come loose from its bun, and hung in sodden strands around her face.

"Jacqui alerted on this, based on the scent she got from the sock the counselor retrieved from Olivia's dirty laundry bag," Anna said.

"We'll know for certain once we get results from the lab," the sheriff said. He nodded to Jake. "You can bag it now."

Wearing gloves, Jake picked up one edge of the shirt between thumb and forefinger and lifted it. "That looks like it was slashed with a knife or a razor or something," Shane said.

No one else said anything as Jake placed the garment in an evidence bag. Aaron wondered if they, like him, were focused on the blood.

"What's that on the ground?" Jamie asked. She pointed to what looked to Aaron like colored string, pressed into the mud where the torn shirt had lain.

The sheriff used a pen to tease the item from the mud. "It looks like colored string, woven into a pattern," he said.

"It's a friendship bracelet," Jamie said. When they all looked at her, she shrugged. "My sister, Donna, is into making them. Girls trade them with each other."

"Olivia's friend Stella was wearing a bracelet like that," Aaron said.

The sheriff placed the bracelet into an evidence bag. "We'll find out if Olivia had a bracelet like this."

"Was there anything else?" Aaron asked. "Any footprints or sign of a struggle?"

"Nothing," Ryker said. "I was with Anna when Jacqui found it and the ground isn't really disturbed at all. It's almost like someone just dropped it there."

"We'll keep searching, keeping in mind that we may be looking for a wounded girl," Travis said, his expression grim. He was a hard man to read, but Aaron knew he had children of his own. Was he thinking of them? He looked at each of them in turn. "We need to talk to everyone who had contact with Olivia in the last twenty-four hours—campers, counselors, other staff at the camp. Anyone who might have seen her with someone or heard her say something that might be relevant." He turned to Aaron. "Did you learn anything from her cabin mate?"

"Olivia had a relationship with a sixteen-year-old boy at home. Her parents didn't approve. They forbade her to see him again and sent her here for the summer to get her away from him. The friend, Stella, says Olivia told her she was mad at the boy and didn't want to see him again, but she may have been lying to cover up a planned meeting. Stella said this wasn't the first time Olivia sneaked out of the cabin after lights out. She thinks Olivia was meeting someone, but doesn't know who, or even if it was a boy or a girl. She did say she had never seen Olivia interact with the boys at camp, or with male staff, outside of the incidental contact you would expect."

"I'll talk to the parents, get the name of this boy and follow up on his whereabouts," Travis said.

He turned and started walking away, but Aaron followed. "There's something else you should know," he said.

Travis stopped and waited. "There's a man on staff here, Gary Reynolds," Aaron said. "He's a maintenance man. A relatively new hire, from what I can gather. I know him. He's from Vermont."

Again, Travis said nothing, waiting for Aaron to elaborate. "I knew him as Gareth Delaney. He worked at a youth camp there, also. He was a counselor. A little girl disappeared there and she was later found in the woods nearby. She'd been strangled. At least two people said they saw her with Gareth shortly before she disappeared. He was arrested and questioned, but there was never any further evidence to link him to the crime. The murder is still unsolved."

"Do you know if he had any connection to Olivia?" Travis asked.

"No, sir. But I thought you should know."

Travis nodded. "Let's find this man and talk to him."

WORD HAD SPREAD that something of Olivia's had been found near one of the cabins, some bit of evidence that hinted at violence. There were whispers of blood, even talk that the search had morphed from one for a live girl to a hunt for a body. Over the course of the day, the search teams had shifted and re-formed, some people taking breaks to warm up inside and change into dry clothes, then heading out with different partners to look in different areas. Some areas had already been searched and were being gone over again, while other groups moved out farther away from camp to comb through the forest and rocky cliffs beyond the grounds of the camp.

Willa joined one of these groups, accompanying Carrie Andrews, Caleb Garrison and Harper Stanick on a hike through dense forest. They scrambled over fallen trees and around massive boulders, and stopped to shout Olivia's name and listen to their own voices echo back to them. They moved slowly, scanning the ground for disturbed leaf litter, shoe prints in the mud, broken branches or blood. None of them were trained trackers, but they tried to notice anything in the dripping landscape that might be out of place. Anything to show that a young girl, possibly frightened, possibly injured, had passed this way.

The rain had stopped an hour before, but everything still dripped moisture. They were quickly as soaked as if they had walked through a downpour, simply from brushing against foliage and walking under sodden branches.

Caleb stopped and prodded at a mound of dirt and leaves.

"Did you see something?" Willa asked.

"Bears hide their kills by partially burying them," he said. "I figure a human killer might do the same."

Willa shuddered, but nodded. Statistics weren't on their side here. If Olivia hadn't run away with a boy or other friend, and if she had been injured by something or someone, the more time that passed, the less likely they would find her alive. No one was saying that out loud—yet—but she was sure they were all thinking it.

She remembered when Rachel Sherman had been found. Willa hadn't been involved in looking for the girl, but everyone she knew was keeping track of the search efforts, constantly scrolling for updates on social media. Willa was at work when a paramedic came in and told them Rachel's body had been found. "I heard she was strangled and thrown in the creek," he said. "One of the cops said she probably died within hours of her disappearance." He made a fist. "They ought to find whoever did that to a kid and give him a taste of his own medicine."

Willa had nodded and agreed with the paramedic. That was before Gary had been arrested. Before she had had to listen to people call for the return of the death penalty for "people like him." So many people had assumed that because he had been arrested, Gary must have done those horrible things to an innocent child. No one seemed to believe her when she protested that her brother was innocent. Not even the man she loved.

Caleb's radio chirped with a message from Danny to return to the lodge. "We're calling the search for the night," he said. "It's too hazardous to keep going in the dark when everyone is exhausted. Go home. The sheriff will decide if he needs us tomorrow."

Willa was crossing the lobby when Bethany caught up with her. "Are you riding back with us?" she asked.

"No," Willa said. "My brother is here. I'm going to catch a ride with him."

"My brother is here, too," Bethany said. "But he's one of the sheriff's deputies, so I'll skip riding with him."

She waved and hurried off. Willa went in search of Gary. She approached several clusters of camp employees, but he wasn't among them. She tried texting him, but got no reply. She was standing in the light from a cluster of cabins when Scott Sprague approached. The events of the day had reduced the owner of the camp to a gray and wilted version of his burly self, his clothes disheveled, color drained by fatigue and the unflattering overhead light.

"Can I help you with something?" he asked.

"I'm looking for my brother," she said. "Gary Reynolds?"

His brows drew together. "You're Gary's sister?"

"Yes. Do you know where he is?"

"The sheriff took him away about half an hour ago."

She swayed—or felt as if she had, though perhaps the only thing that shifted was her perception. "They *arrested* him?"

"I believe they took him for questioning," he said. "Of course, I guess that amounts to the same thing, doesn't it?"

AARON STOOD AT the door to the interview room and studied the man at the table across the room. Gary Reynolds hadn't changed much since the last time Aaron had seen him. He had the same pale blond hair and boyish features. The papers in Vermont had played up the contrast of his cherubic appearance with the horrible crime he was accused of committing.

But Gary didn't look particularly cherubic at the moment. He was sweating and fidgeting in the hard chair across the table from Sheriff Walker. It was the kind of behavior Aaron had been taught indicated guilt. But could this also be the behavior of a man who had been wrongly accused once before, and was reliving his worst nightmare?

"What's your relationship with Olivia Pryor?" the sheriff asked.

"I don't have any relationship to Olivia," Gary said.

"You don't know her at all?"

"I'd never even heard her name before today." He had stopped fidgeting, and looked directly at the sheriff when he spoke.

"But you must have seen her around camp," the sheriff said.

"I work in the maintenance department. I don't have any contact with the campers. And I've only been there two weeks."

"Where did you work before you were employed by the camp?"

"I was unemployed."

"Before that, where did you live?"

"I lived in Vermont." His gaze slid to Aaron. "I'm sure Deputy Ames already told you that. I'm sure he told you the whole story."

Travis acted as if he hadn't heard this. "Is your real name Gary Reynolds?" he asked.

"It is now. I had it legally changed."

"Why did you change your name?"

"Because I was the chief suspect in the murder of a little girl in Vermont. I was released because there was no evidence against me, but my name was in the papers. It's in every story online about a famous unsolved crime. Me and my sister were harassed and threatened by people to the point where moving away and changing our names was the only way to have any peace."

"Why did you move to Eagle Mountain?"

"Because it was two thousand miles from Vermont, and a small town where nobody knew us from before. We hoped to make a fresh start here."

"Why did you go to work for Mountain Kingdom camp?"

"Because I needed a job and they agreed to hire me."

"Did you work yesterday?"

"Yes. I was at the camp from 8:00 a.m. to 6:00 p.m."

"What did you do yesterday?"

"I dug a ditch for a water line."

"All day?"

"Yes. It was a long ditch."

"And you left the camp at six?"

"A few minutes after six."

"Where did you go?"

"I went to the house I share with my sister, Willa." He rattled off the address. "I was there all night."

"She can verify that?"

"Yes." He looked at Aaron again. "You know Willa. She isn't a liar."

"I spoke with her," Aaron said. "She confirmed that Gary was at the house all evening."

"Then why are we even having this conversation?" Gary asked.

"When you saw the photo of Olivia Pryor, did you recognize her?" Travis asked.

"No."

"In two weeks working at the camp you didn't recognize her?"

"They're kids. Little girls. I don't pay attention to them. I'm not that kind of man."

"Is there anyone at the camp who does pay attention to the girls?" Travis asked. "The wrong kind of attention?"

"Not that I've noticed. I'm not there to keep tabs on other people. I'm there to do my job."

"Digging ditches."

"Or changing light bulbs or repairing the ice maker in the kitchen or anything else that needs doing."

"Did you know Trevor Lawson?"

Gary blinked. "Yeah, I knew him. He worked part-time at the camp. He was a good guy. I was sorry to hear he died."

"When was the last time you saw him?"

"The evening before last. We were setting up for the bonfire and he helped."

"How did he seem to you?"

"What do you mean?"

"Was he upset about anything? Did he seem agitated, or depressed?"

"No. He was his usual self. Easygoing. Joking around with his brother."

"Did you see him leave the camp?"

"No. I already told you, I left a little after six when my shift ended. Trevor was there, working." He leaned forward. "Why are you asking about Trevor? Do you think he has something to do with Olivia?"

"I just wondered if you knew him." Travis stood. "You can go now. We'll let you know if we have more questions."

"I need to call my sister to come get me."

"You can wait for her in the lobby."

Deputy Shane Ellis escorted Gary out of the room. When Travis and Aaron were alone, the sheriff said, "Tell me about Gary's sister."

Aaron crossed his arms over his chest, then uncrossed them. He had nothing to hide, yet he felt guilty. "Willa is a nurse at the clinic. She volunteers with search and rescue. Jake Gwynn's wife recruited her."

"You knew her in Vermont?"

The sheriff didn't miss anything, did he? "She and I were in a relationship."

The sheriff considered this. "How did she react when you questioned her about her brother's alibi for last night?"

"She was upset. She accused me of targeting him because of what happened in Vermont."

"Why was he a suspect in that girl's murder?"

"Two campers separately reported they saw him talking to her shortly before she was killed."

"Anything else?"

"We had a profile that pegged her killer as a white male in his late teens or early twenties who worked for the camp. Gary fit that description."

"Anything else? Any DNA?"

"No." At the time they had all been so sure he was Rachel's murderer. Only later did Aaron realize they had been guilty of tunnel vision.

"Do you believe his sister is telling the truth about him being at the house all evening?"

"Yes. Though there's always the possibility he sneaked out of the house after she went to bed. Olivia's cabin mate said Olivia was meeting someone. Maybe Gary arranged to meet up with her later."

"Talk to the neighbors. See if any of them remembers seeing him leaving."

"Yes, sir." He started to leave, then hesitated.

"Anything else?" Travis asked.

"Why were you asking about Trevor Lawson?"

"We got the autopsy report. His toxicology shows a blood alcohol level of twice the legal limit. He had also ingested secobarbital."

"Sleeping pills?"

"Yes. His brother says Trevor didn't take anything like that. Trevor also had a black eye and two broken fingers and a busted lip."

"Injuries suffered in the accident?" Aaron asked.

"The coroner doesn't think so. He estimates they happened a couple of hours before Trevor died."

Aaron frowned. "So, he was in a fight?"

"That's what I'd like to find out."

"I didn't notice any bruising on Gary Reynolds."

"Neither did I. Or Trevor's brother. It's probably unrelated to Olivia's disappearance, but they're both connected to the camp."

"Seems like an odd coincidence."

"It does." Travis moved toward the door. "Go home and get some rest. You can talk to the Reynolds' neighbors tomorrow."

Gary was gone by the time Aaron entered the front lobby. Willa must have arrived to pick him up. It was just as well Aaron hadn't been there to see her. Earlier today she had made it clear how much she hated him.

He got into his car but instead of heading home he drove to the street where Willa and Gary lived. It was too late to talk to the neighbors, but he wanted to see the house. It was a small, square, wooden building on a fieldstone foundation—a miner's cottage, dating from the turn of the twentieth century. The older part of town was full of these small homes, many of them converted to rentals. Willa's car was in the driveway—the same blue Toyota she had owned when they were dating.

He wished he could talk to her. He wanted to explain what it was like to work a serious case, like a murder. The pressure to find the killer. How easy it was to see things one way.

Things that had looked so obvious to him back then weren't so clear now.

This time was different. No one was going to charge

Gary with anything. He wanted to reassure her of that, but she would never listen to him. Hate clouded her view of him.

As for him, he thought he could see her more clearly than ever. She was still beautiful, and passionate—about her job, her volunteer work and her family. But she would never feel that way about him again. He had made a mistake, and he would have to live with the consequences, wanting what they had once had, and could never have again.

Chapter Six

Willa was exhausted, but she had little hope of sleep. Gary had said very little after she picked him up at the sheriff's department, but they needed to talk. She put water on to boil for tea, and took two cups from the cabinet. "Do you want something to eat?" she asked.

Gary slumped at the kitchen table. He looked as bad as she felt. Worse, maybe, pale and heavy-eyed. "No. Though if you've got anything stronger to go into that tea, I'll take it."

She looked in the cabinet until she found a bottle of rum left over from some long-ago recipe, and set it on the table beside him. "Do we need to hire a lawyer?" she asked.

"I don't think so. We can't afford one anyway. Not a good one."

"I could borrow money." She hated the thought, but she would do it for him.

"You don't need to do that."

"How can you say that? You know what happened last time." Those three days when he had been in jail had been among the worst in her life.

"This wasn't like last time." He unscrewed the cap from the rum. "This was different."

The kettle whistled and she poured water over the tea bags in the two mugs. "What do you mean, different?"

"This sheriff is different. I mean, he didn't say much. He listened more than he talked."

She set a mug in front of him. "What did they ask you?"

"The usual. Did I know Olivia? Where was I last night?" He added rum to his mug. "Aaron was there."

Of course he was. "He's probably the one who told the sheriff to question you."

"Probably. He didn't have much to say, though he did tell the sheriff that you verified that I was here all last night."

"That was big of him."

"I always felt bad about busting you guys up. You seemed really happy with him."

"You didn't bust us up. And it's just as well. I got to see his true colors."

"I guess you wouldn't have made a good cop's wife."

But she could have been a good wife to Aaron. If he had been a good man.

"I'll never forgive him for putting you in this position a second time," she said. "When Scott Sprague told me they had arrested you—"

"They didn't arrest me. They questioned me. And not just about Olivia. They asked other stuff, too. They wanted to know if I had seen anyone else with Olivia. And they asked about Trevor." He picked up the mug and eyed her over the rim. "Why didn't you tell me he died? I found out when I showed up this morning that he drove his car into a canyon. They think it was suicide."

"The search and rescue call yesterday morning." She sat across from him and cradled her own mug. "That was a friend of yours?"

"Yeah." He sipped the tea.

"I'm sorry. I didn't know. Why were they asking about him? They don't think you had anything to do with his death, do you?"

"No. At least I don't think so. They were asking when I saw him last, did he seem upset or depressed, stuff like that."

She sipped the tea, not even caring that it scalded her tongue. "I can't believe this is happening again," she said.

"It's going to be okay. No one can say I was with Olivia because I never even knew her."

"Did they say anything else about Olivia? Did they say what they found that had everyone so agitated? Was it something that belonged to her, or some other kind of evidence?"

"They didn't say anything about that. Someone at camp said it was a shirt or something. And that it had blood on it."

"What do the people at camp think happened to her?"

"No one knows. At first, people said she must have run away. Kids do that, sometimes, I guess. But if they found blood..." He shook his head. "There are some bad people out there."

She couldn't do anything to stop those people. All she could do was try to protect the people she loved. The only family she had left.

DANIEL AND SYLVIA PRYOR had the shattered look of people everywhere dealing with loss and uncertainty. They sat in two chairs in the sheriff's office Tuesday morning, untouched coffee cups in front of them.

"Olivia was happy at the camp," Sylvia said. "Every time we talked to her, she was excited about everything she was doing. All the fun she was having." She glanced at her husband. "We hadn't heard her that happy about anything in a long time."

"Her counselor told us she was sent to the camp to get her away from an older boy she was seeing," Travis said.

"Yes," Daniel Pryor said. "He was sixteen. Olivia was barely thirteen. We felt she was too young to be that serious about anyone. We caught her sneaking out to see him and felt we had to do something."

"Olivia was very upset with us at first," Sylvia said. "But she came around. After her first week at camp, I could tell she was really happy. It was like…like we had our little girl back." Her voice broke and she looked away.

"Who is this boy she was seeing?"

"Jared French," Daniel said. "As soon as the camp called to tell us Olivia was missing, I called Jared to find out if he knew anything. He swears he hasn't been in touch with Olivia. His parents believe he's telling the truth."

"And Jared is at his home now?" Travis asked.

"Actually, he and his family are in Michigan, visiting family," Daniel said. "So we know he and Olivia didn't run away together."

"Did she mention any special friends at camp? Other campers?" Travis asked.

"She talked about the girls in her cabin," Sylvia said. "But never any boys."

"She wouldn't have mentioned boys to us," Daniel said. "Not after what happened with Jared." At his wife's wounded look, he added, "She's a teenager. It's what teenagers do. They don't tell their parents everything."

"We questioned her cabin mates." Travis looked to Aaron. "They didn't mention any boys Olivia was particularly friends with."

"Her friend Stella said Olivia never paid attention to any of the boys," Aaron said. "They tried to tease and flirt with the other girls, but Olivia ignored them."

Sylvia nodded, but said nothing.

"Stella also said that starting about two weeks ago, Olivia had been quieter," Aaron said. "As if she was upset about something. And about then is when she began sneaking out of the cabin at night."

"How can that happen?" Sylvia asked. "I thought a counselor slept in each cabin with the girls. Isn't she supposed to prevent that kind of thing?"

No one had an answer for this. Aaron remembered his own teenage years—how devious he and his friends had been in getting around restrictions and rules. They weren't bad kids, causing mischief and getting into trouble. But they had craved independence and tested their limits at every opportunity.

"I talked to Scott Sprague on the phone yesterday afternoon," Daniel said. "He said he keeps a close eye on the campers and he doesn't think Olivia was seeing anyone associated with the camp. He suggested someone from outside might have been coming onto the property."

"We've questioning everyone in and around the camp," Travis said. "We haven't identified any suspects at this point. We're sending out a couple of search dogs again today, and hope to get a drone up to do an aerial search now that the weather is better." He cleared his throat. "There's something else you should know. A search dog yesterday located a slashed T-shirt near the foundation of a storage building. There was blood on the shirt. It's the same blood type as your daughter's. We need a blood sample from one or both of you for DNA comparison."

"Blood?" Sylvia look as if she might faint.

Her husband gripped her hand. "You say the shirt was slashed?"

"With a knife or razor. But there was no blood on the ground in the area, and no blood trail leading away from the shirt. It's possible the rain washed away any trail. At this point, we don't know."

"But Olivia is hurt. She's out there alone somewhere. And hurt." Sylvia began to weep, head bowed, sobbing quietly.

Daniel rubbed her back. "I want to be a part of the search," he said. "If Olivia hears me, maybe she'll come."

"It's better if you and your wife stay together, so that we can notify you as soon as she's found," Travis said. He didn't say the last thing they wanted was for the girl's father to stumble upon her lifeless body, but Aaron knew that's what he was thinking. "Someone can take you to the lodge at camp. You can wait there, nearby. We'd also like you to go through Olivia's things at the camp. You might spot something unusual or out of place that we would miss." This task would give them something else to focus on, and a way to feel useful.

"Of course," Daniel said.

"Deputy Ames will drive you to the camp," Travis said.

"We have our own car," Daniel said.

"Then he'll follow you there," Travis said.

Aaron nodded. Neither he nor the sheriff believed the Pryors had anything to do with their daughter's disappearance, but it was good police procedure to keep an eye on them and gauge their initial reactions to the scene. And deputies were going to question everyone at the camp again, in the hope that this time someone would have something useful to say. Something that would lead them to Olivia.

A CASUAL VISITOR to the camp would have had no clue to the previous day's chaos. The sound of cheerful children's voices echoed among the pines and groups of campers gathered on the shore of the lake or around the cabins. Despite Olivia's disappearance, everything appeared to be operating as usual at Mountain Kingdom.

Aaron escorted the Pryors to Olivia's cabin, and the bottom bunk where she had slept. At the end of the bed was a metal trunk that held her belongings. Her mother sat on the bed and sorted through the contents of the trunk, tears streaming down her face as she smoothed her hand over pajamas and swimsuits, and a stack of green Mountain Kingdom T-shirts, like the one the search dog had located.

"There's nothing unusual here," she said when the trunk was empty, its contents stacked on the bed beside her.

"Did she have a phone?" Aaron asked. Veronica had told him campers were not allowed to have cell phones, but he was curious if Olivia had sneaked one in.

"No, I have it with me." Sylvia dug in her purse and handed him the cell phone.

"Has it been on the whole time?" he asked.

She shook her head. "I switched it on after we found out she was missing. In case she tried to call." She bit her lip, holding back tears.

"Could you unlock it for me, please?"

She unlocked the screen and returned it to him. He scrolled through the history. No calls in almost a month, and before that calls to home and someone named Sara. "Who is Sara?"

"Her best friend at school."

He had to scroll back two more weeks to find a series of text messages to Jared—a furious discussion of her parents' anger and threats to tear the young lovers apart. Then a gap of a few days and an angry exchange in which Olivia said she was glad they broke up and she never wanted to see him again. That fit with the story Stella had told them.

He returned the phone. "Thank you for looking through these things. I'll take you to the lodge now."

"I can do that." Scott Sprague crossed the cabin to them. Freshly shaved and wearing pressed khakis and a green Mountain Kingdom polo, he looked less haggard than he had yesterday. "I'm sure you have questions for me," he told the Pryors. "I'll do my best to answer them."

"I have a question for you," Aaron said. "Are you intending to keep the camp open while Olivia is missing?"

Scott looked puzzled. "I don't think it's wise to disrupt the children's lives any further. While we don't know yet what happened to Olivia, I'm sure she's merely run away and will be found very soon. And I truly believe, despite this very unfortunate incident, that the children are safer here than almost anywhere. So far, the parents agree with me. Though any parent may remove their child at any time, none of them have elected to do so. I see it as a testament to their faith in me."

Aaron didn't want to point out the possible significance of the bloody shirt with Olivia's parents there, so he merely frowned and shook his head. He didn't think the sheriff could order a private business to shut down, though if he had been a parent in this situation, he would have been retrieving his child as soon as possible.

Aaron left the Pryors with Scott and was headed toward the parking lot when someone hailed him. He turned back to see Gary Reynolds jogging toward him. "I'm glad

I caught you," Gary said and stopped beside Aaron, a little out of breath.

"What is it?" Aaron asked. He braced himself for anger. Maybe Gary wanted to berate him for telling the sheriff about Rachel's disappearance and Gary's role as a suspect.

But Willa's brother didn't appear angry. "I've found something," he said. "Something you need to see."

"What is it?"

"Come look."

He followed Gary across camp, around to the back of the mess hall to a small storage shed. "This is a shed where we keep extra canned goods, bottled water and stuff like that," he said. "I came out here this morning to get a case of spaghetti sauce for the cook and saw someone broke the lock." He stepped back so that Aaron could move in closer. The padlock which had fastened the door was intact, but the wood around it was splintered.

"I think they broke it with that crowbar." Gary pointed to an iron bar that lay on the ground nearby.

"Is anything missing?" Aaron asked.

"I don't know. I didn't want to touch anything until someone official got a look. But I know it wasn't like this yesterday."

Aaron nodded. Yesterday they had searched this area multiple times. Someone would have seen this damage. He took out his phone and snapped half a dozen photos of the door and the crowbar on the ground, then put on a pair of gloves. "Let's take a look inside."

He eased open the door and peered into the dark space. "There's a pull chain for a light overhead," Gary said.

Aaron tugged on the light. "Notice anything out of place?" he asked.

Gary shouldered his way into the small space. "That case of water wasn't open last time I was in here." He indicated a flat of water bottles, the plastic wrapping on one corner pulled back and three bottles missing. He moved farther into the space, toward the back. "There are bins back here where they store extra blankets and sleeping bags. The lid is off one of them and it looks like someone rifled through here. And there's some backpacking equipment that hangs on the wall. There's an empty spot where I think there might have been a pack. You'd have to ask the counselors what was in it."

Aaron joined him and took more photos, then they both backed out of the building. "What time did you get to work this morning?" Aaron asked.

"My shift starts at eight. I got here a few minutes before, parked and walked up to the mess hall for a cup of coffee. The cook asked me to fetch the spaghetti sauce, so I got the key from her and came back here and found the lock busted. I saw you walking across to the parking lot and thought I'd better have you take a look."

Aaron nodded. "Thanks."

Gary shifted from foot to foot, hands shoved in the pockets of his jeans. "Should I be worried?" he asked. "Willa says we should hire a lawyer. Should we?"

"I talked to your neighbors this morning," Aaron said. "The woman across the street says your truck was parked at the curb all night. Her kid was sick with a stomach virus and she was up and down all night and she could see it out of her front window. She's pretty sure Willa's car was there, too."

"So you're saying my alibi holds up."

"We had to question you. We wouldn't be doing our jobs if we didn't."

"You guys in Vermont wasted a lot of time with me. They never found who killed Rachel."

"No, they didn't."

Gary kicked a rock. "What is with these people, hurting little kids?"

"I don't know. We don't know Olivia is hurt. Maybe she took these things and ran away."

"I heard they found a shirt of hers. With blood on it."

"Where did you hear that?"

Gary shrugged. "People talk. And what about Trevor? Did he really kill himself? He didn't seem the type."

"What's the type?"

Gary sighed. "Yeah. I guess you never know. It just seems weird, him dying, then Olivia disappearing."

"Maybe she ran away because Trevor died. Maybe he was the person she was meeting when she sneaked out of the cabin."

"I don't know anything about that."

Aaron would talk to Trevor's brother again. Maybe there was something there. It didn't explain the ripped shirt or the blood, but it was something…

"How did Willa seem, when you talked to her?" Gary asked.

Aaron stared at Gary, surprised. "What do you mean?"

"Was she different from before?"

"She still hates my guts, if that's what you're asking," Aaron said.

Gary shook his head. "Did you notice she's thinner? And just, I don't know, sadder. I mean, I get that what happened, with Rachel and me being arrested, and then all the people who thought they could solve the case hassling us, was really awful. But when she decided we should change our names and move here, I thought it would be a good thing. A fresh start. She got a good job, then joined search and rescue. Guys ask her out all the time, but she won't say yes to any of them. She just seems, I don't know, stuck."

"She's been through a lot," Aaron said. Had he hurt her so badly she would never recover? "All this happening isn't helping any."

"Seeing you again upset her lot," Gary said. He shifted again. "But it got me thinking."

"About what?"

"You don't get upset about something you don't still care about."

"She cares about you," Aaron said.

"She does. But at one time she cared about you. A lot."

Aaron's throat tightened, making it difficult to speak. "Those days are gone." He forced out the words.

"I don't know about that," Gary said. "I mean, you have to wonder why we ended up here, in Eagle Mountain. Willa says she forgot that you had family here, but I wonder."

Aaron's radio crackled and Gary took a step back. "I have to get to work, but I'll be around if you need me."

Aaron keyed the mic and responded to a summons to meet the sheriff at the lodge. He needed to report the broken lock and the theft from the storage shed, but instead his mind raced with what Gary had told him. Did Willa still care about him? He certainly hadn't seen it in her eyes last time they had spoken. At one time he would have said he knew her better than almost anyone in the world. Now she was a stranger to him.

As for whether or not he still cared about her…it was a question he didn't have to think about very hard to know the answer. Willa would always be the one he measured every other relationship against. That didn't strike him as

particularly healthy or well-adjusted, but it was the truth.
She may have grown to hate him, but his heart had never
let go of her.

Chapter Seven

Willa worked at the clinic all day Tuesday, checking her phone every hour for updates. Volunteers were still searching for Olivia, but the efforts were more targeted. Danny said the sheriff's department had launched a drone. They had brought in a second tracking dog, but they were having no luck picking up Olivia's scent, possibly because of the rain since she had disappeared.

At noon, she texted Gary to ask how he was doing. He replied OK, then refused to respond to further texts. He didn't like to be nagged, but she couldn't help it. Her mind kept replaying the nightmare of him being hauled away in handcuffs, outside their house in Vermont. Gary might have convinced himself that wasn't going to happen again, but she didn't have that kind of faith.

A little after four o'clock she was updating a patient chart when her phone buzzed with a search and rescue alert. Before she could respond, a call came in from Danny. "You're going to get an alert about a fallen climber," he said.

"It just came through," she said.

"I'm tied up here in Junction. And Dr. Rand Martin, our medical director, is in surgery. I know you're at the clinic today, but is there any way you can get free? It sounds like this climber is going to need medical attention and while there are plenty of people who can assess him and give the appropriate care to stabilize him until he can be transported, if he needs pain meds it's better if we have a licensed person on-site."

"Of course." She stood and began gathering her belongings. "We're not that busy, and there are people here who can cover for me."

"Thanks. Let me know how it goes."

She told her supervisor what was up and got permission to leave work early, texted Gary to let him know she might be home late and set out, grateful to have something new to focus on, even temporarily. Someone she didn't know was having what was probably one of the worst days of his life. She could help make that day a little bit better.

SCOTT SPRAGUE STUDIED the damage to the storage room door, unspeaking, then moved into the center of the small space. "I can't say for certain whether anything has been taken," he said. "When the counselors need things like water or a sleeping bag or pack, they're supposed to log what they take, but that doesn't always happen." He indicated a clipboard hanging by the door.

Aaron peered at the last listing on the board. "The last entry is dated two days ago. Someone took two bags of marshmallows for the bonfire."

"Employees wouldn't have broken the door to get in, would they?" Travis asked.

"They'd better not," Scott said. "You say Gary Reynolds reported this to you?"

"Yes."

"He should have told me first, and I would have notified you."

"I was nearby when he discovered the damage," Aaron said. "I think that's why he came to me first."

Scott said nothing. He exited the shed and Travis and Aaron followed. "Are you any closer to finding Olivia?" Scott asked.

"We're still searching," Travis said.

"But you're not finding. She's one little girl. How far could she have gotten in a rainstorm? You should have found some sign of her by now."

"Unfortunately, there are a lot of places to hide in this rugged country. A lot of places to get lost."

A lot of ways to get hurt, Aaron thought, but didn't say it out loud.

"You took Reynolds in for questioning," Scott said. "What did you find out from him?"

"Nothing," Travis said.

"He's my newest employee," Scott said. "I don't know much about him. Seems suspicious this girl disappears right after he shows up."

"Do you think he knew Olivia?" Travis asked.

"What do her friends say?"

"They don't remember ever seeing her alone with a staff member or even another camper," Travis said.

"Kids are good at hiding things. And they don't always tell the truth." Scott spread his hands wide. "Don't get me wrong. I love kids. It's why I run a kids camp. But they're not all little angels. You can't believe everything they say. Or don't say."

"Have you considered temporarily closing the camp and sending the children home?" Travis asked.

Scott's expression hardened. "I don't think you understand what a thin financial margin I operate on here, Sheriff," he said. "Closing the camp would be utter disaster for

Mountain Kingdom. We might never recover. Of course, if I believed the children were in any real danger, I wouldn't hesitate to send them away. But I really don't see how petty vandalism and one missing girl—who probably ran away—is a serious threat."

"Not everyone would agree with that assessment," Travis said.

"I've run this camp for decades," Scott said. "I know how to keep my campers safe."

The sheriff held his gaze for a long moment, but Scott didn't blink. "We'll let you know if we find anything," Travis said.

They left Scott contemplating the damaged door. "I want to talk to Wade Lawson," Travis said.

They found Wade with a group of boys and girls in an open-air pavilion, where they were working on some kind of leather craft. "Can we speak with you a minute?" Travis asked.

"Sure." He caught the eye of the woman across from him. "I'll just be a minute, Veronica."

He followed Travis and Aaron to a tree some distance away. "What's up?"

"We got the coroner's report back on your brother," Travis said.

Wade's expression tightened. "What did it show?"

"He had over twice the legal limit of alcohol in his system. And he had taken sleeping pills. A couple of them, at least. Seconal."

Wade shook his head. "Trevor didn't take sleeping pills. He wouldn't hardly even take an aspirin. He didn't like pills of any kind. And he never got drunk."

"Never?"

"I can think of maybe two or three times in his life I

ever saw him even tipsy. And he wouldn't drink and drive. Besides, when I saw him at the bonfire, he was perfectly sober and happy."

"He didn't argue with anyone that night?"

"No! What makes you think that?"

"He had a black eye, two broken fingers and a busted lip," Travis said. "The coroner thinks all those injuries happened several hours before he died."

Wade stared. "Somebody beat him up?"

"Have you seen anyone around here with bruised knuckles or any injuries like that?" Aaron asked.

"No." He took a deep breath, then looked Travis in the eye. "None of what you're describing is anything Trevor would do. Do you think someone could have kidnapped him, beat him up, filled him full of pills and alcohol, then forced him off the road? Because that's the only thing that makes sense to me."

"Who would do that?" Travis asked. "And why?"

"I can't figure it out. It sounds like a movie plot or something. But I can't believe he would kill himself. I know people probably say that all the time but Trevor really wasn't like that. He was a happy guy. And if something was bothering him, I would have heard about it. He wasn't the type to keep things to himself."

"Did Trevor know Olivia Pryor?" Aaron asked.

"Do you think this has anything to do with what happened to Olivia?" Wade asked.

"Did Trevor and Olivia know each other?" Travis asked.

"I don't think so. I mean, I never saw him talking to her or anything." He rubbed the back of his neck. "When he started working here part-time, I made a big deal about how he had to stay away from the kids, especially the girls. You don't ever want to be alone with them, or touch them, or do anything somebody might misconstrue. That's a sure way to get in big trouble. I harped on it a lot and Trevor took the warnings to heart. He was friendly, but not too friendly. Mostly, he just helped me out and focused on the job."

"We haven't found any connection between Olivia and your brother," Travis said.

"I hope they find her soon," Wade said. "She was a good kid. Polite. Smart. Her parents must be sick about this."

"We're not going to stop looking for her," Travis said. "Call me if you think of anything helpful."

"Yeah, sure. Thanks."

Wade returned to the crafts session, and Travis and Aaron headed for the main lodge. "We're sending the drone up again this afternoon," Travis said. "And tonight we've got a military helicopter flying over with heat-sensing technology. If she's out there, maybe they'll find her."

Aaron sensed the worry behind his words. The sheriff wasn't known for talking. Right now it was as if he was listing out loud everything they were doing to find Olivia, listening for anything he might have left out or overlooked.

"Tell me about the girl in Vermont," Travis said. "The one who was killed."

Aaron paused, gathering his thoughts. "Rachel Sherman was nine," he began. "She disappeared right after dinner. She was on her way back to her cabin with four friends and stopped to use the toilet. They went on without her. She never showed up at the cabin, so the counselor sent a couple of older girls to look for her. They couldn't find her, so she alerted the camp manager. A search was conducted by camp staff, then they called the police department. We searched and the next day found her body up under some brush on a creek about half a mile from the camp. She had been strangled. Sexually molested, but there was no DNA."

"And no idea who killed her?"

"None. There were rumors there had been a man camping in the area, but we never found him. It's always hard when you don't solve a case, but when it's a kid…"

Travis nodded. "I'm going to talk to the Pryors again. Maybe they can help me learn more about what kind of kid Olivia is. How she thinks. If she was attacked by someone and got free, where would she go?"

"Why wouldn't she run to someone in authority in the camp?" Aaron asked. "One of them could have called us right away."

"That's what I need to figure out."

INSTEAD OF DRIVING to search and rescue headquarters, Willa headed straight to Caspar Canyon, a popular rock climbing area where her patient was reportedly stranded on a rock face with a possible broken leg. Tony and Caleb were already there, and half a dozen other volunteers soon arrived. Climbers gathered around them.

"He was almost to the top when something went wrong and he slipped," an agitated man in a red climbing helmet said. "He was trying to hold on, but he slid about forty feet down the wall and landed on that narrow ledge." He pointed up to the sheer rock face above them.

There were several ledges that didn't look wide enough to hold anyone. Willa couldn't tell where the injured climber lay, but Tony said, "I see him."

"I was up top and looked down and could see his leg was bent at this awful angle," the other climber said. "And he was just screaming and screaming." He swallowed. "That stopped. I think he passed out or something. I thought about trying to get down to him, but I was afraid I might push him off the ledge trying to get to him."

"We need to come down from the top and lower him to here," Tony said. He started giving orders, using terms Willa couldn't understand.

"What can I do to help?" she asked.

"I'll radio you as soon as I get to him with a report on his condition," Tony said. "You can talk me through what I need to do."

She stood back and waited as others moved in to rig ropes and pulleys and assemble gear. Tony left and moments later appeared at the top of the cliff, descending toward the narrow ledge where Willa could just make out a slumped figure. No one spoke as Tony moved down the face of the rock. She found she was holding her breath as she watched him make the descent. Could she ever do something so risky to help someone she didn't even know? She had joined search and rescue primarily to lend her medical expertise, and her license that allowed her to prescribe and administer certain medications. But she had told Danny on her first day that she wanted to go through the regular training, like any rookie. She wanted to be a working member of the team, not merely someone on the sidelines.

When Tony reached the ledge, he hovered beside it for several moments before perching on the edge, leaning back against his ropes for balance.

Willa's radio crackled. "His leg's at a forty-degree angle in the wrong direction," Tony said. "I'm going to cut open his pants to get a better look." There was a ripping sound, then a loud moan. "Easy," Tony said. "I'm with search and rescue. We're going to take care of you." More moaning and the brush of fabric against rock. "Not a compound fracture," Tony said. "I need an air splint for this leg. I'll need to straighten it and that's not going to be any fun for either of us. His shoulder is injured, too. I can't tell how much.

It's going to take two of us to get him into a litter and lower him down. He could use some pain meds."

"I'll send up an injection for him." She got more information about his approximate weight, then retrieved the lockbox of drugs and drew up the appropriate dosage of painkiller. She placed this in a plastic case that snapped shut and handed it off to Ryan Welch, who was going to make the descent with the air cast and other first aid supplies.

A tense half hour followed. Ryan reached the other side of the ledge and handed off the painkiller. Tony gave the injection and they waited for it to take effect, talking with the semiconscious climber and doing their best to make him comfortable. Then they worked together to get the injured leg in the air splint and assess the shoulder. Willa listened in as they relayed details about the climber's medical condition, and she was able to suggest some things they could do to make transport easier. Then they began the awkward task of moving him from the ledge to a litter, first fitting him with a cervical collar and strapping the shoulder to immobilize it.

A Rayford County Sheriff's Department SUV escorted the ambulance into the canyon. Willa stiffened, then let out a sigh of relief when she saw the deputy was not Aaron, but a woman. She introduced herself as Deputy Jamie Douglas.

"How's it going?" Jamie asked, and nodded toward the suspended litter.

"They're getting ready to lower him down," Willa said.

One of the paramedics joined them. "What have we got?" he asked.

Willa explained the situation and what they had done to care for the man, including all medications administered.

"Sounds like all we need to do is get him to the hospital," the paramedic said.

It seemed to Willa to take forever for the man to arrive safely on the ground, though by her watch only another twenty minutes passed. Ryan and Tony descended alongside the litter, keeping it steady and helping it over any outcroppings. By the time everyone was on the ground, Willa noticed the men were sweating from the exertion.

"You did a great job," she told them.

"He's going to be okay," Tony said as they watched the paramedics load the climber into the ambulance. "Thanks for your help."

"You did all the hard work," she said.

"Everyone's contribution matters," he said.

She stayed to help load equipment, then headed home, feeling calmer than she had all day. It had been good to focus on something else for a while. To remember that hers were not the most pressing concerns in the world.

She drove toward home, but on the edge of town found herself behind a familiar black pickup truck. Her gaze focused on the sticker on the left side of the bumper, advertising a popular Waterbury restaurant. She studied the driver's silhouette through the truck's rear window. She would know that erect, dark-haired figure anywhere. She let her foot off the gas and slowed. The last thing she wanted was for Aaron to think she was following him.

But when he put on his blinker and turned onto a side street, she found herself making the turn also. Two-thirds of the way down the street, he headed into the drive of a dark brown A-frame and parked. She sped past, catching a glimpse of him getting out of the truck as she did so. The house was small, like hers. A rental? Or had he purchased it? Did he live there alone, or with a roommate? A woman? The idea that he might be living with a woman made her stomach twist.

Not because she was jealous. But maybe because it hurt to think he had gotten over the pain of their parting so easily.

She gripped the steering wheel harder and made the block and headed home. What Aaron Ames did with his life was none of her business. All she cared about was taking care of Gary and herself.

She was surprised to see that Gary's truck wasn't in the driveway. He almost always got home before she did. Once inside, she texted him. Everything OK? But he didn't answer.

He's probably out with friends, she told herself. Except that Gary hadn't gone out with anyone during their short time in Eagle Mountain. He wasn't the type to party and almost always came straight home from work.

Half an hour later, she called his phone, but it went straight to voicemail. She was on the edge of panic. Had the sheriff picked him up again?

With trembling hands, she searched for the nonemergency number for the sheriff's department, but her call went to voicemail. She hung up, then tried to think what to do. She could go to the sheriff's department, but was anyone even there after hours? Or rather, was there anyone there who would let her in?

She stared at her phone again. She had deleted Aaron's number from her contacts a year ago, but she could still remember the digits. She dialed it, only to have an unfamiliar woman answer. That shook her. Did he had a girlfriend? A wife?

"Is Aaron there?" she asked.

"Aaron don't have this number anymore," the woman said, and hung up.

Willa tucked the phone away. She didn't know Aaron's

new number, but she did know where he lived. And she was desperate to make sure Gary was safe.

Aaron's truck was still in the driveway of the A-frame. Willa parked her Toyota behind it, then forced herself to get out and walk up to the door. She knocked and waited for an answer.

She was about to turn around and retreat to her car once more when the door opened. Aaron, barefoot and shirtless, wearing only joggers and the St. Michael medallion his mother had given him when he became a police officer, opened the door. His dark hair was damp and he smelled of herbal shampoo and shaving soap. She had a horrifying vision of walking right into his arms and resting her head on his shoulder, surrendering to the comforting sensation of his strong arms around her.

"Willa? Is something wrong?"

She stared at him, embarrassment heating her face. What was she doing here? "I… I can't find Gary," she said. "I thought maybe…maybe you had arrested him again."

He stepped back, and the door opened wider. "We haven't arrested Gary," he said. "Come in and I'll help you find him."

She followed him into a small living area. He picked up a T-shirt from the end of the sofa and pulled it on. She stared, distracted by the ripple of his back muscles as he pulled the shirt over his head, but unable to look away. When he turned to find her watching him, her face heated again.

"Why did you think we had arrested Gary?" he asked.

"Because that's what happened before. You took him in for questioning and let him go, but the next day you arrested him."

"That was a different case," he said. "Sit down. Please." He sat on the sofa and motioned for her to join him. Instead, she perched on the edge of a chair across from him. "You told the sheriff about what happened in Vermont," she said. "You told him to question Gary."

"We questioned a lot of people from the camp," he said. "We're still questioning people. The more people we talk to, the more likely we'll learn something useful."

"Is Gary a suspect in Olivia's disappearance? He didn't even know her."

"He's not a suspect. A neighbor confirmed his alibi and we haven't found any connection between him and Olivia. Unless you know something he hasn't told us."

"No." She shook her head. "You double-checked his alibi? You didn't believe me?"

"It's not about what I believe or don't believe," he said. "All that matters is what a jury believes. Two witnesses are always better than one."

"Like the two girls who said they saw Gary talking to Rachel before she disappeared."

"Two witnesses would have been more convincing than one, yes."

"But not convincing enough for the DA to prosecute."

"We didn't have a strong case. All we had was an FBI profile and the statements of those two girls. It wasn't enough. I don't think the sheriff here would even have arrested your brother."

"Then why was he arrested in Vermont?"

He leaned forward, elbows on knees, his gaze locked to hers. She wanted to look away, but she couldn't. He spoke softly, but his words held an intensity that had her leaning toward him. "The police chief was under a lot of pressure to solve the case. All of us were. I'm not saying that to excuse what was done, only to try to help you see what was going on behind the scenes. We didn't have anything to go on. No suspects. Then we had Gary. He fit the profile. He had been seen with Rachel. The sheriff thought if we questioned him long enough, he would crack."

"You mean, he would confess."

"Yes. But he never did."

"Because he wasn't guilty!" She clenched her fists.

He reached out and put a hand over hers. "I see that now," he said. "I didn't see it then. I'm sorry."

She stared at his hand, the feeling of its weight and warmth so familiar. She told herself she should pull away, but she couldn't.

"I'm sorry this has hurt you so much," he said.

Was that *pity* in his voice? The idea repelled her. She pushed away. "We didn't leave Vermont because we were running away," she said. "We left because we didn't have a choice. Not if we wanted to have any kind of life. I tried so hard to find anyone else who might have killed Rachel. There were rumors of some guy living in the woods near the camp, but by the time the police looked for him, he was gone. I tried to find him. I even hired a private detective, but he couldn't find anything."

"We weren't even sure there was a guy in the woods," Aaron said. "It sounded like the kind of story that kids make up to scare themselves around the campfire."

"Did you even look for him?" She couldn't keep the bitterness from her voice.

"We did," he said. "I personally spent half a day out there, searching for some sign of a camp. But there wasn't anything."

"Until they find who really killed Rachel, Gary will always have that hanging over his head," she said. "Every true crime podcast that rehashes the case mentions him."

"Unfortunately, some cases are never solved," he said.

"Especially when there's so little evidence, as in Rachel's case. I'm sorry."

Did she believe him? What difference did it make if she did?

"I'm afraid it will be the same thing all over again if Olivia isn't found safe," she said. "Did they really find her blood?"

He straightened, and pulled his hand away. "I can't say."

"I think that probably means yes."

"We're doing everything we can to find her," he said. "That's the most important thing right now. If she's alive, she can tell us herself what happened."

"And if she's not alive?"

"Then maybe she'll still tell us what happened, through the evidence at the scene."

She nodded, and bowed her head, suddenly so exhausted.

"Why Willa Reynolds?" he asked. "Your new name, I mean? Why did you choose that one?"

"Oh." She took a deep breath, trying to pull herself together. "Willa was my mom's name. Reynolds was my dad's middle name. It seemed a good way to still remember them, but it's the kind of thing it would be harder for a random person on the internet to figure out. At least, I hoped so." She sighed. "Gary didn't want to change his name at all, but I persuaded him to go by Gary instead of Gareth, and he agreed to Reynolds because at least it was still connected to our dad."

"And Eagle Mountain? How did you end up here?"

"I could get a job here," she said. "I answered an ad I found in a nursing publication. And it was a long way from Vermont, but it had mountains."

"Still, it seems like a big coincidence, both of us ending up here."

"The name of the town in the ad caught my attention," she said. "I didn't remember until later that Bethany had moved here and you raved about how beautiful it was. I guess the name stuck in my head. But I didn't know *you* were going to move here." She stood. "I should go."

He rose also, and moved toward her. She thought at first he was going to pull her to him, and she flinched. She didn't trust herself in his arms. She was too aware of him—the scent of him, the memory of his touch. He wasn't good for her, but her body wasn't paying any attention to that knowledge. Every part of her ached for him and she didn't know, right now, if she was strong enough to resist him. "I can help you look for Gary," he said.

She shook her head and pulled out her phone, and saw to her surprise that she had a new text message. She opened it. I'm home, Gary had texted.

"Gary's home," she said, shaky with relief.

"Good." Aaron still wasn't touching her, but he stood so close she could see the gold flecks in his brown eyes and the dot of shaving cream just beneath his left sideburn. Her gaze shifted to his mouth, and her own lips parted. Then their eyes met and she felt pulled to him.

He stepped back, and turned away. "Are you all right now?" he asked.

Would she ever be all right again? She felt wrung-out. Drained. "I'm fine," she said, and forced herself to move past him, toward the door.

She didn't remember walking out the door or to her car. She didn't even remember driving home, though she was soon there, parking behind Gary's truck. The conscious part of her was still back there with Aaron. Waiting for his kiss. Wanting it as much as her next breath.

Chapter Eight

Tuesday was Aaron's father's birthday, and nothing short of a genuine emergency could excuse Aaron and his siblings from their presence at the family table. "Everyone is pulling extra shifts right now, trying to find this missing girl," Aaron said when his mom called to remind him he was expected for the birthday celebration. When they weren't actively scrutinizing the countryside for any sign of the missing girl, they were combing through evidence for any clue as to her whereabouts.

"You still have to eat," his mother said. "If you can't join us, I'll bring a plate to you at the sheriff's department."

Aaron could only imagine the ribbing he would endure if his mother showed up with dinner for him. Though some of it would probably be jealousy—Diane Ames was a good cook. "I can stop by for a little while," he said. "But I have to eat and run."

Thus, he found himself in his usual seat at the family table, across from Bethany and her fiancé, Ian. Aaron hadn't been so sure about the professional mountain climber—and reputed billionaire—when they had first met. He had been afraid the guy would end up hurting Bethany, who had a tender heart and a history of poor judgment when it came to men. But he had been happy to admit he was wrong.

Ian had proved to be a stand-up guy and he truly seemed to care about Bethany.

Twins Carter and Dalton sat on either side of Aaron—two years younger than him and showing no sign of settling down. They worked as drivers, tour guides and general handymen for the family business, Peak Jeep Tours and Rentals. Their parents—married thirty years and still doing everything together—were at either end of the table, which was loaded down with lasagna and a huge salad, a basket of bread sticks and a lemon birthday cake for dessert.

"A group of us are getting together to search those gullies and caves on the back side of Mount Wilson tomorrow afternoon," Carter said as he doused his salad in dressing.

"I'll help," Ian said. An internationally known climber, Ian Seabrook had settled in Eagle Mountain to open a via ferrata, a public climbing route.

"We should ask Willa to come with us," Bethany said. "I know she wants to help, and I'd like to get to know her better."

"Yeah, I want to meet her," Carter said. "Every search and rescue call she's been on, I haven't had a chance to speak to her. I hear she's really good-looking."

"I noticed her watching you, Aaron," Bethany said. "She was really checking you out."

Aaron forced himself not to react. "When was that?"

"When we responded to the call about the guy who drove off Dixon Pass. And again at the youth camp, that first day we searched for Olivia. Willa couldn't take her eyes off you. You should definitely ask her out."

He shook his head. "That's not going to happen."

"Why not?" his mother asked.

He debated lying but the truth was going to come out.

"Do you remember the woman I was seeing in Vermont?" he asked. "Kat Delaney?"

"I remember her," Carter said. "The two of you broke up after her brother was arrested for the murder of that little girl at the summer camp."

"What murder?" Bethany asked. "And the woman you were dating was named Kat?"

"Short for Katherine," Carter said. "And this little girl at a summer camp in Waterbury was murdered."

"You had already moved away when all that was going on," Dalton said.

"What about her?" Carter asked. He stabbed at his salad. "You can't ask Willa out because Kat broke your heart?"

"I can't ask Willa out because she *is* Kat." He shoveled a forkful of lasagna into his mouth and chewed, though he might as well have been eating packing peanuts.

"What?" Carter paused, fork halfway to his lips. "Willa and Kat are the same person?"

Aaron nodded and swallowed. "I guess she and her brother were harassed so much they moved and changed their names. They had no idea I was living here."

"If Willa is Kat, why didn't I recognize her?" Carter asked.

"She was out of context," Dalton said. "We didn't expect to run into Aaron's ex here. Plus, the name change threw us. And we never got that close to her."

"Still, makes me think I'm losing my touch." Carter returned his focus to his food. "I usually have a good memory for good-looking women."

"So do you think her brother did it?" Dalton asked. "Killed that girl? And does he have anything to do with Olivia's disappearance?"

"The charges were dismissed because we didn't have any

real evidence against him," Aaron said. "Just a couple of girls who had seen him talking to Rachel earlier in the day, and he fit the FBI profile. At the time, the sheriff thought he was acting guilty, but he was probably just scared."

"Yeah, but what does your cop instinct tell you?" Dalton asked.

Aaron shook his head. "I don't know if I believe in 'cop instinct.' At the time, I convinced myself he was guilty, because that's what everyone around me said they thought. Now—I don't think he was."

"What a terrible thing to happen," his mother said. "I can't imagine having to change my name and move all the way across the country to start over, just to get away from a scandal like that."

A scandal Aaron had helped to set in motion. Whatever Gary may or may not have done, Kat—Willa—was innocent. But she had suffered just as much as her brother had. She was still suffering.

This afternoon, when he had opened the door to find her there, it had taken all his will not to pull her close. She had looked so shaken and afraid. And when he had dared to touch her he had felt the connection like an electrical current. He had looked into her eyes and thought she felt it, too. The connection and the longing to be together again.

Then he had realized he was letting his emotions lead him in the wrong direction. Willa hadn't come to his home for help. She had come to accuse him of arresting her brother. That was still how she saw him—as the enemy. The person who had ruined her life.

So he had done the only thing he could see was right and let her walk away. She would never know how much that had cost him. He turned to Carter. "Do me a favor, and don't ask her out," he said. He doubted Willa would say yes—not when she realized who he was. But no sense taking chances. The only thing worse that not having Willa would be seeing her with his brother. "And don't say a word about her name change."

"I won't," Carter said. For once his brother wasn't making a joke out of the situation.

"Let me get this straight," Bethany said. "Kat—who is now Willa—broke up with you because her brother was suspected of murdering this little girl at the summer camp. Except now you don't think he did it, and in any case, he was never charged with the crime. And now your former girlfriend and her brother are living in Eagle Mountain, with new names."

"Yeah." Aaron looked down at the remains of his lasagna; his appetite vanished.

"Wow," Bethany said. "Of all the places for her to end up. Maybe it's because the two of you are meant to be together after all."

"That's not how life works, Bethany," Aaron said.

"You only say that because you're a cop," Bethany said. "But there are people who believe—"

"Bethany, did you look at those bridesmaids dresses in the link I sent you?" his mother interrupted.

Aaron guessed after so many years of raising four children his mom was an expert in heading off an argument. And he really didn't want to argue with his sister about fate and destiny and all that nonsense. He and Willa had been good together, but now she hated him and he had to learn to live with that.

"I did, Mom." Their mother couldn't see it, but Aaron didn't miss the conspiratorial look Bethany sent Ian. "We're thinking of something a little simpler."

"Some of those dresses were quite plain," his mother said.

"Yes, but we're looking or a more rustic wedding venue. We want to keep it very casual."

"I don't see why you can't have the wedding in a church and the reception in the canyon," his mother said.

It was an old argument. One his mother was not going to win. Bethany had defied her parents to see Ian and that had given her all the courage she needed to stand firm on her wedding plans. Good for her. But Aaron didn't want to get involved. He slid back his chair.

"I have to go now," he said. "Thanks for the dinner, Mom. It was great."

"But you haven't even had dessert. It's lemon Italian cream cake—your father's favorite."

"And we have to sing 'Happy Birthday' to Dad," Bethany said.

"Think I'll skip the cake tonight." He patted his flat stomach. "Have to stay in shape."

He lingered long enough for "Happy Birthday," then he left, back to the side of his life he felt better equipped to handle. He might not solve every crime, and they were no closer to finding Olivia after two days of intense searching, but he knew how to investigate and dig and the next steps he should take. Relationships—whether romantic or familial—were a lot more unpredictable.

WILLA'S FIRST PATIENT after lunch on Wednesday was a camper from Mountain Kingdom who had fallen on a hike and broken her arm. Juliet was twelve, with a cloud of curly red hair and a gangly frame. She had a tear in her shorts and tears running down her face, but Willa praised her for being brave and talked about what a great story she would have to tell her friends back home, and eventually coaxed a smile from her.

After X-rays and an examination by the nurse practitioner, Willa presented Juliet with a lollipop and set about casting the injured arm. While this was being done, the counselor was called into the business office to complete some paperwork.

Willa watched the woman leave, then asked, "Did you know Olivia, the girl everyone is looking for?"

"Uh-huh. But I don't know what happened to her." Juliet licked the lollipop. "The adults keep asking everyone over and over, but we don't know anything." The girl's voice rose, and Willa looked nervously toward the office. She could see the counselor's back from here. Could the woman hear how upset her charge was becoming? Willa was liable to be reprimanded for meddling in something that wasn't her concern.

"I'm sorry about your friend," she said, and applied the last of the wet plaster. "How does that feel?"

"Funny. Is it going to itch?"

"It shouldn't itch too much. Is it too tight?"

"I don't think so." She met Willa's gaze, her expression serious. "I don't know Olivia that well," she said. "But her best friend at camp, Stella, is really upset. I heard her crying in her bunk last night, and I think it was because of Olivia. Or maybe it's because she sprained her ankle. But I don't think that's it. The ankle is all wrapped up and Stella told me it hardly hurts at all anymore. And she gets to skip all the hikes and stuff. But she also has to miss out on swimming, so maybe she's just sad about that." Juliet shrugged. "Some kids cry all the time, especially the little ones who get homesick, but Stella isn't like that, so I figure she just misses Olivia."

"I imagine she does."

"How are we doing?" The counselor returned to the

room. She frowned at Willa. Had she overheard part of the conversation?

"Would you like pink, orange, purple or green for the final layer?" Willa asked, and showed the box of colored wraps.

"Purple," Juliet said.

Ten minutes later, the counselor and the girl left, the child showing off her purple cast.

The door opened and Aaron entered. Willa stiffened. "How can I help you, Deputy?"

"Would you be willing to go to lunch with me? Just to talk."

This wasn't the first time she had been asked out in front of a waiting room full of patients. She had even heard a rumor that there was a secret betting pool on how long it would be before the new nurse agreed to go out with someone. She was used to turning men down with a minimum of fuss, but Aaron's invitation caught her off guard. What made him think she would even consider going out with him?

But she remembered those moments of connection the other night at his house. She had wanted to believe those feelings were all one-sided. Apparently not, and he had gotten the wrong message. "I don't think that would be a good idea," she said, keeping her voice low.

He nodded, showing no disappointment or surprise at her rejection. "Could you answer a medical question for me?"

Almost everyone in the waiting room was watching the two of them, not even pretending interest in anything else.

"Come back here," she said, and led the way to an empty exam room. She closed the door behind them, then thought perhaps she shouldn't have. The room was small, and suddenly intimate, with the two of them so close together.

"What kind of medical question? Are you sick?" The idea alarmed her. He looked healthy. Better than healthy—he looked perfect. But you couldn't always tell…

"I'm trying to figure out how you could give sleeping pills to someone against their will," he said.

Not what she expected. "Do you have someone in mind?"

"It's a hypothetical. It's related to a case I'm working on."

"All right. Well, there are lots of ways. You could crush them up and put them in food or a drink. How many pills are we talking about?"

"Two or three."

"Depending on what you put them in, the person you're giving them to might not even notice."

"This person didn't have any food in their stomach."

"Then I'm not sure how you would do it."

"Could you force the pills down their throat? The way you'd pill a dog or cat?"

"I suppose so. If they were restrained."

"Could you do that with alcohol, too? Pour booze down their throat?"

"Not without choking them." She knew better than to ask him for details. She had learned very early in their relationship that he took privacy concerns very seriously. As did she. She didn't talk about her patients, and he didn't talk about his cases. It hadn't mattered, because they had so much else to talk about—books, music, news and life itself. She had been a little smug at times. One thing she and Aaron did well was communicate, and that was supposed to be the key to a good relationship, wasn't it?

"I suppose you could make someone drink anything if you threatened them with a weapon," she said. "Or threatened someone they loved." The idea made her queasy. "Who is doing these horrible things?"

"I'm not sure anyone is doing anything. At this point, I'm just speculating."

"Does this have anything to do with Olivia?" she asked.

"No. This is something else. And don't tell anyone we had this conversation. It's so far-fetched they'd probably laugh me off the force if they knew. I was just curious." He moved a little closer, his tone confiding. "To tell the truth, it gave me an excuse to talk to you. I've missed that."

She had missed it, too. But that didn't mean it was a good idea to spend too much time talking with him. "I have to get back to work," she said.

"Me, too." But he lingered, his gaze like the brush of his fingers across her skin.

A knock on the door made them both jump. "Willa, is everything all right? You have a patient ready."

She glanced up at him, a desperate look, and he stepped aside and opened the door. She rushed past him and hurried toward the examining room, fleeing her own worst impulses.

Jake radioed as Aaron was leaving the clinic. "What's your twenty?" Jake asked.

"I'm headed back to the sheriff's department. I'm about a block away."

"Do you have time to run back out to Mount Wilson Lodge with me? Dwight has something he wants to show us."

"Sure. What's he got?"

"He didn't say. He wants us to take a look and arrive at our own conclusions."

They met at Jake's sheriff's department SUV. He looked as exhausted as they all did, worn out but determined to keep going, desperately hoping for some sign of that missing little girl. Every day that passed made it less likely they would find her alive. Gradually the case was moving from a rescue mission to a search for a body to give the family closure and, they hoped, provide more clues to what had happened.

Aaron might have dozed on the drive out to the fishing and hunting lodge. He snapped to as they turned in at the gate. Dwight met them in front of the lodge with two quad-runners. "This is the best way to get to where we need to go," he said.

Jake got behind the wheel of one vehicle, while Aaron rode with Dwight in the other. They headed down a trail, past a large lake where two men stood, fly-fishing.

"The wife of one of those guys went hiking this morning," Dwight said. "When she came back she asked me about this place. I couldn't really figure out what she was talking about, so after she went back to her cabin, I rode out here to take a look. That's when I decided to call this in."

"Call what in?" Aaron asked.

"It's hard to describe. You'll have to see and decide for yourself." Past the lake, he turned off on another trail that led up an incline to the east. "We're headed toward Mountain Kingdom Kids Camp now," Dwight said.

"How far is the camp from here?" Aaron asked.

"About a mile as the crow flies. A little farther on foot. It's pretty rough country—a lot of blow-down trees and big boulders scattered around. Some of the search and rescue people came through there the day Olivia was reported missing. They didn't find anything, but it would have been easy to miss someone in that kind of terrain."

They threaded their way through dense forest, then across a high meadow, until they reached a three-strand barbed wire fence. Dwight stopped and shut off the machine. Jake parked beside him.

"We have to walk from here," Dwight said. "We'll be on national forest property."

"How did your hiker end up out here?" Jake asked as he ducked between the strands of barbed wire.

"She said she was following a trail that just stopped," Dwight said. "I think she must have gotten off on a deer trail. Fortunately, she has a good sense of direction and was able to find her way back to the fence and the main trail from there." He pulled out his phone. "I marked the GPS coordinates after I found what she was talking about."

They walked for another hundred yards, Dwight frequently consulting the screen on his phone. They detoured around a thick stand of aspen, then came to a stop.

"What are we looking for?" Aaron asked.

"Over there." Dwight pointed to what at first looked like a clump of brush. But as Aaron moved closer he could see it was actually branches that had been bent over, the ends weighted down with rocks to form a tunnel.

He crouched down and looked inside. "Did you go in?" he asked.

"No. Look there, just inside. Do you see it?"

Jake moved in to peer over Aaron's shoulder. "It's a shoe print," he said. "A small shoe print."

Aaron studied the faint outline, as if from the sole of an athletic shoe. "About the size a thirteen-year-old girl might wear," he said.

"My guest didn't notice that," Dwight said. "She was asking me what kind of animal made the tunnel."

Jake and Aaron looked at each other. "One of us has to go in there," Jake said. "In case she's in there."

"I'll do it," Aaron said.

"Let's photograph that shoe impression first." Jake took out his phone. "And the structure, too, in case you tear it up."

Photographs taken, Aaron prepared to crawl on his hands and knees down the narrow tunnel. It was a tight fit, and branches scraped his back in several places, but after approximately four feet he emerged into a larger space. "It's like an igloo made of branches," he said. He could hear Dwight and Jake just outside. An igloo just big enough for one half-grown person to shelter.

"Is anyone in there?" Jake called.

"No. But the grass is all pressed down, like someone was sleeping here." He studied the ground closely and spotted a blue label. He placed this in an evidence envelope, then retraced his path down the tunnel.

He was grateful to stand upright once more, his back protesting as he straightened. He handed the evidence bag to Jake. "I found this. It's the same brand of water as the ones taken from the Mountain Kingdom storage shed."

Jake looked back at the tunnel. "Do you think Olivia was hiding out here? Why?"

"Maybe she wanted to prove she could?" he guessed.

"When I was a kid I read a series of books about a kid who lived alone in the wilderness after a plane wreck," Dwight said. "I used to daydream about doing something like that, but I never would have really tried it."

"I read those books, too," Aaron said. "Maybe Olivia did, too."

"That doesn't explain the bloody shirt," Jake said.

"No, it doesn't," Aaron said. "Unless that shirt is the reason she's hiding. She's afraid whoever did that to her is still after her." He looked around then. "You would have to be right up on this place to ever see it."

"Smart kid, to figure all this out," Jake said. He pulled a coin from his pocket. "You want heads or tails?"

"What for?" Aaron asked.

"The loser waits here while the other one goes back to Dwight's house and calls it in. We'll have to get forensics, see if we can find any definitive evidence that Olivia was here."

"She was here," Aaron said. "No adult made this. Everything about it is kid sized."

"Heads or tails?" Jake repeated.

"Heads."

The coin came up tails. Aaron settled in to wait while Jake and Dwight returned to the lodge. After a while he sat, his back against a tree, warm sun on his face. For the first time in days, he felt at peace. This wasn't a place where someone had been held captive. This was a hideout. A safe place. Olivia had been here recently; he was sure. And she was alive.

The only questions were why had she hidden out here, and where was she now?

Chapter Nine

"We're asking search and rescue to assist with an intense, targeted search in this section of national forest between Mountain Kingdom Kids Camp and Mount Wilson Lodge." Sheriff Travis Walker stood before the gathered search and rescue volunteers Wednesday afternoon inside the main building of the Mount Wilson Lodge. He indicated a section outlined in red on an enlarged map pinned to the wall. "We've found some indication that Olivia Pryor has been in this area recently."

A murmur rose among the volunteers. "What did you find?" Bethany asked, addressing the sheriff.

"We're passing around a smaller copy of the map," Travis continued. "On the back is a photograph of a brush shelter where we believe Olivia spent at least one night. The location of this shelter is marked on the map. Keep your eyes open for similar primitive shelters like this."

"How would a thirteen-year-old girl know how to build something like this?" Dr. Rand Martin, Eagle Mountain Search and Rescue's chief medical officer, asked.

"Mountain Kingdom has a three-day wilderness adventure course where they take the kids out and teach them survival techniques, including building shelters," Sergeant Gage Walker, the sheriff's brother, spoke up. "Olivia's parents also say she is a big fan of adventure novels and TV shows. Looks like she was paying close attention."

"Do we know why she ran away from camp?" Danny asked. "Can we expect her to try to hide from us?"

"We don't know why she left camp," Travis said. "And yes, she may try to hide. But she's been out there three days now and may be ready to return, if not to Mountain Kingdom, then to her family."

"May I say something, Sheriff?" Scott Sprague stepped forward. The camp owner had added a silver Stetson to his khaki-and-polo uniform, the hat mimicking those worn by some members of the sheriff's department. "Thank you all for volunteering to help with the search for Olivia," he said, his voice projecting clearly in the large room. "All we want is for her to be safe. Whatever reason she decided to run away, it wasn't because of anything that happened at the camp. We know she was happy there."

"Already working on covering his reputation," Carrie Andrews, on Willa's right, whispered.

Scott continued, talking about the illustrious history of his family's camp, and reminding everyone that this was the first time anything like this had happened. The gathered volunteers exchanged glances and shuffled their feet.

"Thank you, Mr. Sprague." Gage put a hand on the camp owner's arm, silencing him. "Let's get out there and start searching. We want to take advantage of every bit of daylight."

Willa turned away, but found herself face-to-face with Carter and Dalton Ames.

"Hi, Willa." Carter offered his hand. "I don't know if you remember us. We're Aaron's brothers. We saw each other a few times in Vermont, but I didn't recognize you until Aaron told us about your name change."

"Of course." She shook hands with each of them in turn. What was she supposed to say? "Um, this is a little awkward."

"Don't worry," Carter said. "We won't tell anyone your secret identity."

She winced. "Thanks."

"Aaron told us the whole story," Dalton said. "Sorry you were being harassed back in Waterbury. And it's great that you joined search and rescue."

"Yeah. If you need anything, let us know," Carter said. He glanced over his shoulder as someone called his name. "We just wanted to say, no hard feelings or anything."

"Yeah." Dalton clapped his brother on the shoulder. "We'd better go."

Willa stared after them. She had a memory of Aaron's brothers as friendly but involved in their own world. All her focus had been on Aaron. At least they didn't hold any grudges about the way she had ended her relationship with their brother.

Willa was assigned to search with Bethany and Carrie. "I saw you talking with Carter and Dalton," Bethany said as Willa approached. "I hope they didn't embarrass you or anything."

"No." She glanced at Carrie, who was studying her phone screen. "They just welcomed me to search and rescue."

"Aaron made them promise not to ask you out," Bethany said.

"No! They didn't ask me out." Aaron had told them that? Why? Of course, she would never have agreed to go out with them. Talk about awkward! "What else did Aaron say about me?" She couldn't help it—she had to know.

"Well…" Bethany looked over to see that Carrie had

turned away and was talking with another volunteer. Then she leaned closer to Willa and lowered her voice. "He said he doesn't think your brother had anything to do with that little girl's murder back in Vermont, that he was only acting guilty because he was scared."

Willa stared. Why couldn't Aaron have seen this at the time of Gary's arrest? Why change his mind now, when it was too late to undo the damage?

Bethany shrugged, maybe reading the unanswered questions in Willa's eyes. "He's not one to admit he's wrong very often."

Carrie turned to them. "We'd better get started."

As they moved out of the building, a fourth person joined them. Aaron, dressed in jeans and a black T-shirt, held up a copy of the map. "I'll be with you three," he said. He looked at Willa, then away. He couldn't have overheard her conversation with his sister, but she still felt the impact of Bethany's words. Aaron had admitted he was wrong about Gary, but wasn't that too little, too late?

"You're out of uniform," Bethany said to her brother.

"We thought the uniforms might scare off Olivia." He slipped a daypack onto his back and glanced at Willa again. "You're the trained professionals. I'm here to follow your lead."

Carrie turned the map over and studied the photograph of the shelter. "They really think Olivia built this thing?" she asked.

"I saw it," Aaron said. "It was really clever."

"Why would a kid go to all that trouble?" Bethany asked. "The camp looks like it would be a blast. Was Olivia secretly bullied or something?"

"No one we talked to mentioned anything like that,"

Aaron said. "The other girls in her cabin seemed to really like her."

"I heard the same thing," Willa said. When they all turned to look to her, she added, "We had one of her cabin mates in the clinic yesterday. She said Olivia's best friend at camp really misses her."

"Her poor parents," Carrie said. "I hope we find her soon."

They set out for the section of the map they were assigned to search—a brush-choked half acre of forest bisected by a deep gully. It was easier to forget about Aaron's close proximity as they fought their way over and around the massive, rotting trunks of fallen trees, pausing to look under each one in case Olivia had hollowed out the space for shelter.

After forty-five minutes of this, they stopped to drink water and catch their breath.

"I don't see how a kid could get through all of that," Bethany said.

"She would probably have an easier time of it than us," Willa said. "She's smaller and probably more flexible."

"It would be a good place to hide," Aaron said. He looked around them. "We're making so much noise thrashing through here, she would hear us coming from a long way off. All she would have to do is double back to an area we had already searched and wait until we left."

"Come on out, Olivia!" Bethany shouted. "Your parents really want you to come home!"

Aaron was leaning against the same tree trunk as Willa, two feet of space between them. "Did the girl you saw at the clinic have anything else to say about Olivia?" he asked.

"She said she didn't know Olivia very well, but that her friend Stella cries at night now that Olivia is gone. She thinks it's because Stella misses her friend." She couldn't believe she was having a regular conversation with him. It didn't even feel that awkward. They were behaving like normal people, no messy past between them.

"We've still got a lot of ground to cover," Carrie said. "We'd better get going."

Another half hour of pulling aside thorny vines, slipping in mud and scrambling up rocks had Willa feeling bruised and battered. She stood atop a granite boulder and surveyed the surrounding wilderness. Then her breath caught.

"There's someone over there!" she said, and pointed straight ahead.

Aaron vaulted up beside her, and steadied himself by briefly holding her arm. He released his hold and followed her gaze. Someone was clearly moving around, ducking under branches and around rocks.

"There aren't supposed to be any other searchers assigned to this section," Carrie said.

Aaron cupped his hands around his mouth. "Hello!" he shouted.

The figure stopped. Aaron took a pair of binoculars from his pack and focused. "It's not Olivia," he said. He handed the binoculars to Willa.

She focused in on a burly older man in a green shirt and a silver Stetson. "It's Scott Sprague," she said.

Aaron waved. "Mr. Sprague!" he shouted.

Scott looked up, then began picking his way toward them. "What are you doing out here by yourself?" Aaron asked when Scott was almost to the boulder where they waited.

"I can't sit still and do nothing while Olivia is missing," he said. "I'm responsible for that little girl."

"It isn't safe to be in this rough country alone," Aaron

said. "You need to go back to camp and leave the searching to us."

"It would be terrible if you were hurt while you were trying to help," Carrie said. "The camp needs you."

He slumped against the rock. "You're probably right. I felt energized when that brush shelter was found. Now that we know that Olivia is alive and probably close by, it feels wrong not to be out here searching for her."

"I'm sure you're a big help to Olivia's parents," Bethany said. "You should go back to them."

He wiped a hand over his face. Up close, Willa could see slashes from vines across his cheek, and scraped knuckles on his hands. He didn't even have a pack or water. She pulled one of her own water bottles from her pack. "Drink this," she said.

"Bethany, could you go with Scott back to camp?" Aaron asked. At his sister's frown, he added, "Please?"

"I don't want to take one of you away from the search," Scott protested. "I'm sure I can find my way on my own." He looked around. "If you'll start me off in the right direction."

"I'd better go with you," Bethany said. "It's so easy to get turned around out here." She consulted the map. "It's going to be easier to retrace our steps to the lodge. Are you ready, Mr. Sprague?"

"Please, call me Scott." He returned the half-empty water bottle to Willa. "And I'm ready, thank you."

Bethany and Scott headed back the way they had come, and the other three pushed forward once more. Willa was more aware now of Aaron staying close to her. Once, when she lost her balance on a rolling log, he took her elbow to steady her. He released her as soon as she was secure, but she hadn't flinched from his touch.

"Thanks," she muttered, and moved on.

She slowed down after a moment, and let him get in front of her. She liked being able to watch him as he broke a trail through the thickest brush. The black T-shirt emphasized his muscular shoulders and arms. He wore a gun in a small holster on his hip, a badge clipped beside it. Even though he was out of uniform he was still on duty, she reminded herself.

"Do you remember the day we climbed Mount Hunger?" he asked.

She groaned. "That last mile was so hard. I was beginning to wonder if you were trying to get rid of me."

"But the view at the end was worth it."

"Yes." The end of the hike offered a spectacular view of the surrounding mountains. But it wasn't the view she remembered most—it was the kiss they had shared, and the euphoria of having conquered something difficult together. She had never felt closer to anyone in that moment and had been sure she could face anything with this man. But that feeling had been a mirage. They had climbed that mountain together, but when the most difficult thing she had ever endured in her life happened, Aaron wasn't beside her; he was opposing her. He was the one responsible for her problem.

THEY HAD COVERED every inch of their search area by 6:00 p.m., and returned to the lodge dirty, bruised and worn-out. The other searchers looked the same. No one had found any sign of Olivia.

"Maybe you were wrong about that shelter," Bethany said when she found Aaron eating dinner catered by the lodge. She slid onto the picnic table bench beside him and helped herself to a potato chip from his plate. "I was talking to Scott and he said that wilderness course they take the kids on didn't have anything about building brush shelters, just instructions on basic first aid and how to use a compass and the importance of staying put if you're lost."

"There was a shoe print just inside the shelter," Aaron said. "The same size as Olivia's foot. And a label from the same brand of water bottles we found in camp."

"That's something, I guess." She ate another chip. "You were sticking pretty close to Willa today," she said. "Does that mean the two of you are going to get back together?"

"Not much chance of that." He crunched a chip. "I'll settle for her tolerating my presence."

"Oh, I think she more than tolerates you," Bethany said. "She was checking out your butt when you were hiking ahead of her."

He laughed, at the disgusted expression on his sister's face as much as at the idea that Willa had been ogling him. "Don't tell me you don't check out Ian's backside sometimes," he said.

"Well, yeah, but that's different. Ian isn't my brother."

"I'm not Willa's brother, either." And he wasn't exactly her friend. He hoped he wasn't her enemy. It wasn't all he wanted from her, but it was better than he had hoped for.

Jake approached the table, plate in hand. "Do you have room here?"

"Sure." Bethany scooted over to allow him to slip in beside her. "Where were you searching?"

"I was with a group searching the area where we found the shelter." Jake bit into a sandwich and chewed.

"I guess you didn't find anything," Bethany said.

He shook his head.

"I wish we knew why she ran away," Bethany said. "If we knew that, we might have a better feeling for where she would go. I mean, is she trying to get away from someone or to someone—or something?"

"Good question," Aaron said. Why hadn't he thought of that?

"If she was in that shelter, she didn't go that far from camp," Jake said.

"And that water and stuff was taken from the storage shed after she was reported missing," Aaron said. "So she was still close to camp, then."

"It's like she's sticking around to see what happens," Bethany said.

"If she's just playing a game, it's time to stop," Aaron said.

"There's still that shirt with the blood on it." Jake spoke quietly. He cut his eyes to Bethany. "And you didn't hear me say that."

"It's not a secret," she said. "But it's good to hear the rumor confirmed." She leaned toward them and spoke in a whisper. "Was the blood really Olivia's?"

Jake nodded.

"So, somebody hurt Olivia, she ran away and now she's hanging around," Bethany said. "Maybe she's waiting for the person who hurt her to get caught. When they are, she'll come out of hiding."

"Then it would help if she would leave a few more clues as to this person's identity," Aaron said. He pushed his plate away. "And that sounds awful. She's just a kid. Maybe hurt. Probably frightened. She's not supposed to have to do our job for us."

"There's no other DNA on that shirt," Jake said, still speaking quietly. "So we have no idea who might have attacked her."

"You would think one of the other campers would know

something," Bethany said. "I mean, girls talk. Boys, too. They can't help it. They never stop. I remember going to a Girl Scout camp for two weeks when I was eleven. It was nonstop talking. By the end of the week I knew the darkest secrets of at least a dozen girls I would never see again. I knew whose parents were getting divorced and whose big brother had a drug habit and who had a creepy uncle they avoided being alone with at family gatherings. If Olivia had a secret, somebody must know it."

"No one's telling us anything," Aaron said. "We've questioned all the campers more than once."

"You two are cops. And you're men. And you're old. I mean, you're not old, but to a young teen anyone over twenty-five might as well be their parents."

"Do you think they'd tell you anything they wouldn't tell us?" Aaron asked.

"Maybe. Though by this point they've already either outright lied to you or just omitted to mention something important. And they've probably done it more than once. Which means they're even less likely to volunteer information to yet another stranger. Even a female who's not a cop." She paused, then turned to Aaron. "You could ask Willa to talk to them."

"Why Willa?" Jake asked.

"She's a nurse. Nurses are used to getting information out of people in a nonthreatening way. She's pretty. Girls like that. And she looks younger than she is. I think they would be more likely to trust her."

"It's not a bad idea," Jake said. "Though I'm not sure how we'd square it with Scott. He might not like the idea of bringing in another outsider when there's so much focus on a missing camper. I've heard some parents are questioning whether he's doing enough to protect the campers.

They're questioning staff qualifications and security measures and things like that. A new person interacting with the kids might draw attention he doesn't need right now."

"It's something to think about." Bethany stood. "I have to go. Some journalist is coming tomorrow to write up a feature about the via ferrata. I'm supposed to put together a press kit for her."

She left. "Do you think Willa would talk to the girls in Olivia's cabin?" Jake asked.

"I think she would do anything to help find Olivia," Aaron said. "But how would we ever make it happen?"

"Maybe she could volunteer to teach a first aid course at the camp."

"I'm sure they already have someone to do that."

"They probably don't have a nurse," Jake said. "And Bethany's right—Willa is pretty. Scott Sprague strikes me as a man who might be influenced by pretty."

"What makes you say that?"

Jake shrugged. "I was watching him that first day, when all the searchers were at camp. He wasn't exactly leering at some of the women, but he was definitely aware of them."

"Like most men," Aaron said.

"Talk to Willa. See what she thinks about the idea."

"Why should I be the one to talk to her?"

Jake gave him a pitying look. "You're not fooling anyone, Aaron. We've all seen the way you look at her. You might as well talk to her. Maybe you can even work the conversation around to asking her out. Though I'll warn you, she's turned down better men than you. Supposedly there's a pool at Mo's about how long it will take before she agrees to go out with the many men who've worked up the nerve to ask her."

Aaron could have told Jake he was certain he wouldn't

be the one to win that lottery. Instead, he merely shook his head. "I'll ask Willa about proposing a first aid course for the campers, but don't blame me if she says no. Should we talk to the sheriff first?"

Jake considered this. "Probably not. He won't want to involve a civilian. If Willa does it and learns anything useful, she can pass it on as a concerned citizen and leave us out of it."

"Coward."

"Says the man who's afraid to talk to a beautiful woman."

Aaron scowled. He wasn't afraid of Willa—only fearful of ending the fragile peace between them.

Chapter Ten

The search and rescue volunteers were preparing to leave Mountain Kingdom when an alert came in from the 911 operator. "A woman called in, says her husband is injured, with a possible broken leg," the operator told Danny as the team listened in. "She says he's fallen into some kind of trap and can't get out."

"A trap? Like, a bear trap?" Danny frowned.

"She says it's a hole in the ground, with branches over it to hide it. He fell in and she thinks he broke his leg. I have GPS coordinates for you."

"All right. Go ahead." Danny nodded to Tony, who was standing next to him, and Tony took out his phone, prepared to enter the coordinates.

The dispatcher rattled off the numbers and Tony typed them in. "That's pretty close to here," Tony said. "Less than a mile away, down a different county road." He frowned at his phone screen. "It's not near any established trail."

"What were they doing out there?" Danny asked the dispatcher.

"The woman says they were looking for that missing little girl."

"Tell them we're on our way." He ended the call and turned his attention to the assembled volunteers. "Those of you who want or need to go home, do so," he said. "You've been out here all day. We only need about six people to handle this."

"I'll come," Willa said. Going home meant hours of sitting and worrying. Better to be active and help someone in need.

"I'll go, too," Ryan said. "I want to see this trap."

Tony, Vince Shepherd and Ryan's fiancée, Deni Traynor, made up the rest of the crew that set out toward the area where the couple was stranded.

"We'll have to hike in from here," Tony said, enlarging the area map on his phone.

Danny distributed first aid supplies, including a wheeled litter, splints, back, neck and leg braces, supplemental oxygen and fluids, as well as ropes and other gear for retrieving their patient from the pit he had fallen into. "Some of this is probably overkill," he said as he helped Willa stuff her pack with more bandages. "But we don't know the extent of his injuries and we have to be prepared for the worst."

They set out with Tony in the lead, breaking trail where there was none. The terrain looked like the country they had searched all day—pine and aspen forest pocked with boulders and gullies, choked with deadfall and impenetrable thickets of scrub oak. Tony had a machete to cut a path where absolutely necessary, but mostly they tried to detour around smaller obstacles, alert for hazards and for any sign of Olivia.

It took an hour to reach the couple. They heard them before they saw them, the woman calling out, "Over here!" and a man's very loud "Thank you!"

The group stopped at the edge of a small clearing and stared at the scene before them. The woman stood beside a boulder and looked from the group to a hole in the ground.

The hole was approximately six feet across, with green pine branches piled around it on two sides. Moving carefully, Danny led the way to the edge of the pit.

The man was approximately five feet down, on his back in the bowl-like depression on a bed of more green branches. The scent of pine perfumed the air. "We were walking along, taking our time, searching for any sign of the little girl," the woman, a forty-something blonde dressed in jeans, a pink T-shirt and a black day pack, said. "Luke was ahead of me. I heard a scream and looked toward him and he wasn't there."

"The ground gave way and I fell," Luke called up. He wore camo pants and a black T-shirt, a green ball cap over his short, sandy hair.

"Someone spread all these branches over this hole in the ground," the woman explained. "I pulled them away and piled them to the side. Who would do something like that? Were they trying to catch a deer or a bear or something?"

"What's your name, ma'am?" Danny asked.

"Melissa Wagner."

"I'm Danny Irwin. We're going to take care of your husband. It will take a few minutes for us to get down there to him. Meanwhile, you can answer some questions."

While the others helped Tony attach a rope to a sturdy tree nearby and assemble the needed equipment, Danny and Willa questioned Melissa about her husband's medical history and general health. "He said he heard the bone pop when he landed," she said.

"He's pretty sure it's broken, but there's no bone sticking out." She bit her lip, her eyes shiny. "I can't believe someone would do this."

"I've never seen anything like this, either," Danny said. "But right now, let's focus on Luke."

He used the rope to steady himself as he walked down into the pit. Tony and Ryan followed, leaving Deni, Willa and Vince to stay with Melissa and lower supplies via another rope as needed.

"It's like something aboriginal hunters might use," Vince said. "I think I saw that in a book—they dug a pit, lined it with sharp sticks and drove game over it."

"Thank goodness this one didn't have any sharp sticks," Willa said.

"This pit wasn't really dug out," Deni said. "It looks like a tree died a long time ago and the stump rotted away and left this depression. All anyone had to do was scoop out the debris."

She walked a short distance away and stopped beside another downed tree. "The branches they used to cover the hole came from this tree. I can see where someone broke them off."

"They look like they're still green," Vince said.

"The tree has been down a little while," Deni said. "It takes a long time for pine to turn brown."

"Send that oxygen tank down, will you?" Danny radioed.

They returned their attention to caring for their patient, who turned out to have a probable fracture of the fibula and some cracked ribs. They stabilized his injuries, then secured him in the litter and carefully raised him from the pit using a combination of ropes and man power.

At ground level once more, they attached a large wheel to the center of the litter and stationed people at the four corners to steady its occupant and help the contraption over rough places in the ground.

While they were packing up the last of their gear, Ryan took several photographs of the pit and the surrounding area. "We should tell the sheriff about all of this," he said.

"Someone will need to make sure there aren't more of these out here, waiting to trap some person or animal."

"This looks recent," Tony said. "Do you think someone did this to deliberately trap one of the people searching for Olivia?"

"Who would do that?" Deni asked.

"If someone kidnapped Olivia and is holding her around here somewhere, they might be trying to keep other people away," Ryan said.

"Or they could be someone who likes hurting other people for no good reason," Willa said.

Deni put a hand on Ryan's back. "It doesn't matter to us who did this, or why. We need to get Mr. Wagner to the hospital."

They took turns handling the litter. When Willa wasn't involved with that, she sought out Melissa and fell into step alongside her. "Did you see any sign of Olivia before your husband fell?" Willa asked.

"No. We were talking about turning back and going home when Luke fell."

"Why did you decide to search in this area?"

"We want to help, but when we showed up at the camp, they told us only trained search and rescue volunteers were needed there. So we decided to come here. It was close enough we could imagine the little girl might have wandered over." She sighed. "I guess there's a reason they only wanted trained searchers. We didn't realize how rough the country would be. I don't see how a little girl could be okay out here."

"It's hard to want to help and not be able to do anything," Willa said.

"Only now we've made more trouble for everyone."

"It's what we're here for," Willa said. They never wanted

to discourage people from calling for help when they needed it. It was why they didn't charge for rescue missions.

An ambulance was waiting in the parking lot of Mountain Kingdom Kids Camp and they loaded Luke Wagner into it, and Ryan and Deni drove Melissa to her car so that she could meet her husband at the hospital in Junction. Willa, adrenaline ebbing and exhaustion taking over, trudged to her own vehicle at the far edge of the parking lot.

She stiffened when she recognized the tall figure waiting for her. "What do you want?" she asked Aaron, the words coming out more brusquely than she had intended.

"I'm hoping you'll do something to help with our search for Olivia," he said.

She clicked the key fob to unlock her car, but didn't open the door. "What can I do?"

"You could teach a first aid class to the girls in Olivia's cabin. Talk to the kids and see if any of them know something about Olivia and her disappearance that they haven't told authorities."

"Why me?" she asked.

"You're a nurse, so you're qualified," he said. "We think the girls would like you and confide in you."

"Who is 'we'?"

"Me and Jake." He hurried on before she could ask why they had been discussing her in the first place. "The girl you saw in the clinic seemed willing to talk to you about Olivia."

"It seems a sneaky way to get information."

"We've already questioned every camper at least twice," he said. "They're suspicious of cops. They'll be more relaxed with you."

She could see the logic in that. Sort of. "What am I supposed to find out?"

"Why she ran away from camp," he said. "Was someone there bullying her? Was she afraid of anyone? Is she trying to get someone else in trouble? Having those answers might help us figure out how to find her."

She opened the car's rear door and shoved her pack inside. "All right. What do I have to do?"

"You have to persuade Scott Sprague to take you up on the offer."

She made a face. "So he doesn't even know you're planning this?"

"No one knows. Jake and I came up with the idea on our own. Well, with some help from Bethany. She's the one who pointed out that the campers wouldn't want to tell the truth to 'old' men like us."

She almost smiled in spite of herself. "What if Scott says no?"

"Don't take no for an answer." He grinned. "Besides, I don't think he'll turn you down."

"Oh? Why is that?"

"He's a single man. You're a beautiful woman."

She ignored the flutter in her stomach at his words. "You're suggesting I what—*seduce* him into saying yes?"

"No! Nothing like that. Just, you know, smile and make him think you want to do the class as a favor to him—and the campers."

She didn't want to agree to the idea, but she couldn't think of a better one, and she wanted to help find Olivia. "All right, I'll try," she said.

"At least you'll know you tried." He held the driver's door open for her. She gave him what she hoped was a look that told him she didn't need his help, and slid past him, into the seat.

"How did the call go?" he asked. "I heard it was a hiker with a broken leg."

"Fine. We had to pull him out of a hole in the ground he'd fallen into." She was about to start the car, but hesitated, wanting to tell someone about what had happened, and who better than a sheriff's deputy? "Someone had set a trap out there in the woods—a hole in the ground with a bunch of branches over it. This man—he and his wife were out searching for Olivia—stepped on the branches and fell into the hole."

"No pointed sticks at the bottom?" he asked.

She frowned. "No. Vince said something about that, too. I never heard of that."

"It's called a punji trap. They used them in the Vietnam War." At her questioning look, he added, "When I was a teenager I went through a phase where I was really interested in stuff like that. Anyway, someone dug a hole and set up a trap like that—without the sticks?"

"It didn't look like they dug the hole, exactly," she said. "A tree had died and most of it had rotted away. Whoever did this scraped out the rest of the dead tree, then pulled some branches off a pine that had fallen and scattered them around. There's a lot of branches and stuff on the ground around there anyway, so it was good camouflage."

"Was someone trying to trap Olivia?"

"I don't know. It was just…strange." She started the car. "I think Danny is going to contact the sheriff about it. Someone needs to make sure there aren't other traps out there. With so many searchers out in the woods, someone else could get hurt."

He stepped away from the car. "Thanks for agreeing to talk to the kids," he said.

She nodded, and put the car in gear. She didn't like how circumstances kept throwing her and Aaron together.

Most of all, she didn't like how seeing him made her feel—not like she was facing someone who had betrayed her. When she was with Aaron these days, she was reminded of how much she missed him.

GAGE ASKED AARON to come with him to check out the trap that had injured Luke Wagner. They said little as they hiked toward the location search and rescue had provided. Aaron was tired of tramping through the woods, or at least these woods, with their tangled deadfall and uneven terrain. He was constantly slipping on the thick carpet of pine needles or being slapped in the face by low-hanging branches.

"This isn't good," Gage said when they stopped briefly to rest and drink water. He pointed at something on the ground.

Aaron leaned over to look. "Bear scat," he said. There were plenty of black bears in Vermont, though most of his dealings with them had involved chasing them out of people's fruit trees or garbage cans. "Black or grizzly?"

"No grizzlies in Colorado," Gage said. "And the black bears around here usually shy away from people."

"Even if one ran away, it would probably terrify a little girl," Aaron said. The thought made his stomach ache. Forget his own troubles; they needed to find Olivia.

They reached the GPS coordinates they had been given and gathered around the hole in the ground.

"I see what Willa meant when she said this wasn't dug by hand." Aaron indicated the remains of a rotted tree nearby. "Someone used what was already here."

"It looks like they moved some rocks to sort of funnel

traffic this way." Gage pointed at several piles of rocks on either side of a path that led toward the hole.

"They couldn't have known who would end up in it," Aaron said. "Even an animal might have been hurt."

Gage nodded and walked the perimeter of the hole, studying it. "It looks to me like something a kid would do," he said after a while. "My daughter and her friends are always coming up with schemes like this—you know, 'Let's dig a hole in the backyard, fill it with water and make our own swimming pool.' Or 'Let's build a fort by the back fence.' If they came across a big hole in the ground in the middle of the woods, they might remember a scene from a movie or book and decide to re-create it."

"The only kid we think is out here is Olivia," Ryan said. "Why would she do something like this?"

"Maybe she doesn't want to be found," Gage said.

Which again begged the question why. Olivia's parents seemed like decent people who were truly concerned about their daughter. No one had reported Olivia having a bad relationship with her parents. Everyone they had interviewed said she enjoyed camp, though there was Stella's report that Olivia had been sad about something for the past couple of weeks. What would have driven her away from the comforts of the camp to live alone in a rugged wilderness, through a rainstorm, cold nights and the possibility of encountering a bear? It didn't make sense to Aaron.

They took a lot of photos, then marked the spot with orange flags and moved rocks and branches to guide people away from the area.

"That should keep someone else, or any animals, from accidentally falling in," Gage said.

They searched for several hundred yards in all directions around the trap and didn't find anything else suspicious.

"I think someone saw that hole and decided to turn it into a trap on the spur of the moment," Aaron said.

"More kid behavior," Gage said. "Olivia's parents said she was really into outdoor adventure and surviving in the wilderness stories. Maybe this is part of it. Maybe she isn't running away from anything or anyone—she's just out here having fun."

"She has to know people are looking for her. And her parents are worried sick. That's a cruel game. Nothing I've heard about her makes her sound like a cruel kid."

"We won't stop searching for her," Gage said. "It's just something to keep in mind. Our first idea about a situation isn't always right."

Aaron knew that. His former department's first idea about Rachel's killing had been wrong, and look what a mess that had turned into.

Chapter Eleven

Scott Sprague did not turn Willa down when she called and asked to meet with him Thursday afternoon. She arrived for their appointment, not at the lodge, but at the cabin on the property where he lived. He was freshly shaved and smelled of expensive cologne and she immediately doubted her decision to wear a clingy sundress instead of her nurse's scrubs. She wanted this to work, but she didn't want Scott to think she was coming on to him.

He invited her to sit on the porch with him. "I would invite you to join me in the house, but I don't want to start any rumors," he said. "A man in my position has to guard his reputation carefully. Working with children is such a vulnerable responsibility. I can't even risk the appearance of scandal."

"It's a lovely day to sit outside," Willa said diplomatically. From this vantage point, she could see most of the camp—the cabins and mess hall, and the lakeshore beyond. Boys and girls in green T-shirts ran between the trees or clustered around counselors. Several canoes bobbed on the lake, and another group of kids swam in an area marked by yellow buoys.

"You said you wanted to discuss volunteering at the camp?" Scott asked. "We're all trained in first aid, but having a nurse on-site would certainly be welcome."

"I was thinking I could teach a first aid class to the campers," she said. "A couple of hours for each cabin, with hands-on exercises. I find children really enjoy wrapping each other in bandages and trying on slings."

"Our counselors usually do some basic first aid instruction, but it might be good to have a medical professional teach a course." He rubbed his chin. "That would take our training to the next level. Parents would like it. When are you available?"

"We could start tomorrow," she said. Aaron hadn't specified, but it seemed reasonable to her to try to collect information about Olivia as soon as possible. "I have the day off. I could do the girls this Friday and teach the boys next week."

Scott rubbed his chin. "Friday afternoons we have our weekly canoe regatta, but the morning is open." He nodded. "We can sub in your class instead of the pottery workshop. The girls can do pottery next week. Could you be here at nine?"

"Yes."

He stood and extended his hand. "Thank you for offering. We'll see you tomorrow."

She texted Aaron on the walk back to her car.

Class is on for tomorrow. You have to help me figure out what to ask the girls.

He replied right away. When can you meet?

I get off at five.

We need somewhere we won't be overheard, he said.

She hesitated, then typed, Come to my place. Gary

would be there, but that was a good thing. With her brother present, she wouldn't be tempted to let emotion get the better of sense. She didn't exactly hate Aaron anymore, but she would never be foolish enough to trust him.

THIS ISN'T A DATE, Aaron reminded himself as he shaved before meeting Willa Thursday evening. But unmet expectation charged every interaction with her. He was trying to get past that, to accept that the best he could hope for from her was casual friendship. His brain might agree, but his body wasn't listening.

He pulled on jeans and a button-down shirt. Blue—her favorite color. He had jotted some notes, and he carried those with him, adding to the illusion that he was viewing this as strictly business.

She answered the door promptly, still wearing pale blue scrubs from the clinic. "I was running late and just got home," she said. "Would you mind waiting while I change?"

"No problem." He followed her into the house.

"Make yourself comfortable," she said. "Gary should be home soon. I'm going to jump in the shower. I need to wash off any clinic germs."

She hurried away and moments later he heard water running. His mind immediately conjured memories of other showers, ones they had taken together. He groaned and closed his eyes. *Think about something else.* He sat on the sofa and picked up a magazine from the coffee table. *Modern Nursing.* He flipped through it, but could focus on nothing but the running water and the heat coursing through his body.

The back door opened and he stood and moved toward the kitchen. Gary took a step back when Aaron entered.

"Hey," Gary said. "What are you doing here?" He looked

wary, but not hostile. Despite everything that had happened, Aaron had never sensed any particular animosity from Gary.

"I'm meeting with Willa." He held up his folder of notes. His prop to prove there was nothing to see here. No conclusions to leap to.

"Is this about the class she's holding at the camp?" Gary asked. He opened the refrigerator and leaned inside. "Do you want something to drink?"

"No, thanks. Yeah, it's about the first aid class."

"My sister, the police spy." Gary grinned. "Never saw that one coming." He leaned back against the yellow Formica counter.

The kitchen was small and dated—not that different from Aaron's own. But he could see the effort Willa had made to dress it up, with a stained glass piece in the window over the sink, and framed pen-and-ink drawings of fruit and flowers on the wall over the table.

"She's not really working for the sheriff's department," Aaron said.

"Right. It's a big secret." He popped the top on a Coke and sat at the kitchen table.

"Any changes at the camp since Olivia left?" Aaron asked.

"The counselors have to do bed checks every four hours," Gary said. "Whether they're actually doing that, who knows?"

"No more thefts from the storage shed?"

"Nope. It's locked up tight. I take it no one's gotten any closer to finding Olivia?"

"No."

"It's a long time for a girl to be on her own in the wilderness," Gary said. "There aren't many people out there, but there are bears and mountain lions. And what's she doing for food?"

"She may not be on her own. She might have arranged to meet up with someone, or someone might have taken her from the camp."

"Have you seen some sign of another person out there?" Gary asked.

"No, but we have to be open to all possibilities," Aaron said. "That's why I asked Willa to do this. I'm hoping one of Olivia's friends will mention something that will help— if she ever talked about leaving, where she might go, if someone had been bothering her."

"So maybe she didn't just run away?"

"We don't know," Aaron said. "That bloody shirt pointed to violence, but we haven't found any other sign of that. And someone crafted that shelter we found. It didn't look as if it had been there long. It's possible whoever took Olivia made it, but it's just as likely she built it herself. We simply don't know."

Willa came into the room. She had changed into pink shorts and a T-shirt, and had a blue towel wrapped around her head like a turban. "Hey, Gary. How was your day?"

"Okay." Gary stood. "I'm going to leave you two to it."

Willa looked alarmed. "You don't have to leave."

"It's okay. I'm going to check out that new pizza place in town. I heard it's really good." He nodded to Aaron, then left. Willa stared after him.

"Do you really think you need a chaperone?" Aaron asked.

Her cheeks flushed pink. "It's just…awkward."

"It doesn't have to be." He was amazed at how calm he felt. Seeing her nervous made him feel steadier. She wasn't acting like someone who hated him.

"Why don't we sit here?" She indicated the kitchen table. "Do you want something to drink or eat first?" She pulled a can of Coke from the refrigerator and held it up. "Do you want one?"

"Sure."

He accepted the drink, then they sat across from each other and he laid his notes between them. "I should give Bethany credit for this idea," he said. "She thought if we could find out if Olivia was running from something or to something, we could figure out how to persuade her that it's safe to come home – or, if she was kidnapped, it might point to who took her. We're also still trying to determine if she's hurt, and who might have hurt her."

"Because of that bloody shirt?"

"Yes. She's doing a good job of avoiding all the searchers, so that makes me think she's in pretty good shape. We believe she stayed close to the camp for several days at least. We're hoping that's still the case."

"So she wanted to get away, but she stayed nearby. Why?"

"Bethany suggested it's because she's waiting for the person who hurt her to be caught. Then it will be safe for her to return."

"Why not go somewhere and tell someone in authority what happened?" Willa asked.

"I don't know. She seems like a bright kid, but maybe she doesn't feel like she can trust anyone with her secret."

"Or maybe the person who hurt her is someone in authority."

Aaron nodded. "We don't think it was another camper. So that leaves one of the counselors or other workers at the camp."

"Or a parent?" Willa wrinkled her nose.

"We've checked out her parents pretty thoroughly," he said. "There's nothing suspicious there. But you might see if you can find out how Olivia viewed their relationship."

She leaned back and grabbed a legal pad from the counter and began making notes. "Part of first aid is protecting our personal safety and our mental health, too," she said. "With kids, especially, there's an emphasis on not getting into dangerous situations in the first place. That includes identifying people who might be a danger or behave inappropriately. I can start a conversation with the kids from that direction. Maybe they'll mention a particular incident or person at camp."

"That's a good idea," Aaron said. "There's also the possibility that Olivia left on purpose. She wanted to play in the wilderness, see if she could live like people in stories she's read or heard about."

Willa frowned. "That sounds terribly cruel to her parents. Not to mention how she's endangered all the people who are searching for her."

"She probably didn't think about those things."

Willa made more notes. "There will probably be camp employees at my class," she said. "To assist and to keep tabs on me, too. I mean, if I was in charge of a bunch of kids, I wouldn't let any stranger interact with the children without oversight. That might limit how nosy I can be."

"I hadn't thought of that, but you're right. Do the best you can. And maybe you can get a feel for how the adults who are there react to all this talk of inappropriate behavior. You might pick up something we need to investigate further."

"I'm probably not going to find out anything useful," she said. "But at least I can give the kids some first aid skills. I'm taking the class seriously. I'm not just there to be nosy."

"I expected nothing less. You never do anything half-way."

She looked down at her hands—fingers long and delicate, the nails trimmed short and painted pale pink. "I hope that's meant as a compliment."

"One of the things I've always admired most about you is your dedication and loyalty," he said. "If you do a job, you give a hundred percent. If you love someone, you'll do anything for them. Even when you were furious with me over what happened to Gary, I knew it was because he was your brother, and you would do anything to protect him."

"I wouldn't lie," she said. "I always told the truth about him. That's what upset me the most. My alibi for him wasn't enough."

Aaron sighed. How could he make her understand? "We were wrong," he said. "I can say that now. I didn't see it for a long time, though. We were trying to find a killer and on paper—from our skewed point of view at least—Gary looked like the only suspect."

"I've done some reading," she said. "About confirmation bias. Apparently, it's something people don't even realize they're doing."

"I'm glad Gary was released," he said. "And I'm sorry for the hurt I caused you both."

"I wish you would have had the courage to speak up for Gary. To point out how wrong it was to single him out."

They were hard words to hear, but he didn't dodge or excuse the accusation. "I wish that, too," he said. "But at the time I didn't see it."

The silence stretched between them. Was she thinking about how he had pointed out Gary to the sheriff when Olivia disappeared? Could he make her understand that if the sheriff had learned after the fact of the prior accusations against Gary, it would have been a black mark against Aaron's own professionalism?

"As a law enforcement officer, we have to view everyone connected to a case as a potential suspect," he said. "Part of our job is to rule people out. Even though it took a while, the system worked for Gary. There wasn't solid evidence against him and he was released. I know that doesn't happen every time, but it did this time. And here in Eagle Mountain, the sheriff saw right away that Gary wasn't connected to Olivia. Waiting to be ruled out isn't pleasant for anyone involved, but most of the time, the system works."

Are you ever going to forgive me? he wanted to ask, but he couldn't bring himself to beg.

She stood. "I haven't eaten all day. Are you hungry?"

"Yes. We could go out."

She was already removing things from the refrigerator. "I'll cook. Just don't expect fancy."

"When have I ever?"

She turned on the burner under a pan. "Tell me how you ended up in Eagle Mountain."

"You know Bethany moved here first."

"She and her fiancé canceled their wedding," Willa said. "I remember."

"The rest of the family came to visit her after she had been here a few months," he said. "The Jeep tour business where she was working was for sale. My parents decided to buy it and they and the twins all moved here."

"Right. I remember you talked about how beautiful the place was. I think that's why the name of the town caught my eye when I saw the ad for a nurse."

"I came down a second time to help with the move, after you and I broke up, with no intention of staying. But then

I learned there was an opening with the sheriff's department. I interviewed on a whim and they offered me the job."

"Look at you, being impulsive," she said.

"I thought a fresh start might be good." Everywhere he went in Waterbury was filled with memories of her. He thought getting away from that might help him move on with his life. And the change of scenery had helped—until she showed up in town.

Her expression sobered. "Starting over in a new place is hard. But I feel like I'm finding my footing here. Search and rescue has helped. It's good to be part of something bigger than myself."

"Law enforcement is that way, too. The sheriff has a good team here."

She nodded, but said nothing, and focused on cooking.

"Can I do anything to help?" he asked.

"You can get plates from the cabinet and fill glasses with ice water."

Setting the table felt like old times, when he had spent so much time in her home he knew it as well as his own. They had talked of moving in together, and he had planned to propose, when the time felt right.

She served salad topped with grilled chicken, cheese and bacon. "It's delicious," he said.

She laughed. "You always were easy to please."

"Anything you do pleases me."

He hadn't intended to say the words out loud. They had simply slipped out. But he didn't take them back. He looked at her steadily, watching the color bloom on her face, the pupils of her eyes darken. Her tongue darted out to wet her lips.

"Aaron," she said, her voice a little breathy.

I never stopped loving you. But he didn't say it. That would be going too far. Expecting too much.

"I'd like us to be friends," he said instead.

She hesitated, then nodded. "I don't want us to be enemies. But I can't do more."

"I know." Some wounds were too big to get over. He believed that. They finished the meal in silence. When his plate was empty, he stood. "Thanks for dinner," he said. "I'd better go. Let me know if you run into any problems."

"I'll call and let you know what I find out from the kids."

She walked with him to the door. He turned, and started to kiss her good-night, the way he had so many times when leaving her place. Instead, he brushed his lips to her cheek. Not exactly the way he would have kissed his sister, but close enough she couldn't object.

Then he slipped out the door, a picture fixed in his mind of her standing there, one hand to her cheek, staring after him—almost as if she regretted him leaving.

Chapter Twelve

Mrs. Mason greeted Willa when she arrived at camp Friday morning. "Mr. Sprague is sorry he can't be here," she said. "The poor man is spending all his free time searching for Olivia. He's running himself into the ground, he's so worried about her."

"It's an awful situation," Willa said.

"You'll need to sign these." Mrs. Mason handed her a sheaf of papers.

Willa read and signed the documents, which indicated she was not being paid for her services and agreed to comply with a long list of rules for interacting with the children and other camp policies, such as no smoking and no alcoholic beverages. Paperwork complete, she followed the older woman to an open pavilion, where a dozen girls sat at picnic tables.

A counselor, Veronica, sat with the girls. "I can help with anything you need," Veronica said. "I was a life guard in high school and had to take CPR and stuff."

"Thanks." Willa turned to face the children. She had suggested starting with the oldest children first, which meant Olivia's group. She had learned that children older than thirteen attended a sister camp across the lake. "First, I want to learn all your names."

The children took turns introducing themselves, each saying her name and where they were from and if there was anything in particular they wanted to learn. Most didn't have much to say in this regard, though one girl—Kenya—announced that she wanted to learn how to bandage people like a mummy.

Juliet, in her purple cast, was there. And Stella, Olivia's closest friend in the cabin, her ankle no longer wrapped, her brown hair pulled back in a ponytail. Stella wanted to learn how to stop people bleeding. Was this because of the wound of Olivia's that had left blood on her shirt?

Willa began by passing out some basic first aid supplies and letting the girls examine them—bandages, slings, splints and ice packs. They talked about the kinds of accidents they had encountered in camp—burns, cuts, sprains and breaks. "Rodney Carpenter fell face-first on the rocks and knocked out three teeth," one girl volunteered.

"Accidents can't always be predicted," Willa said. "But some can be prevented. The best first aid is the kind you never have to give. What are some of the things you can do to avoid being hurt?"

The girls shared their ideas, from watching where you were going to listening to adults when they told you not to touch things like hot stoves and knives.

"I think we can agree the best way to avoid being hurt is to stay out of dangerous situations," Willa said. "That includes things like wearing a seat belt, not crossing a busy street against the light and wearing a helmet when riding a bike. But it also includes learning to recognize people we should avoid."

"Like people playing with fire and stuff," Juliet said.

"My mother told me if I have a bad feeling about someone, I should stay away from them," Stella said.

"Your mother is right," Willa said. "Not everyone is a good person, so if someone makes you uncomfortable you should stay away from them. And tell an adult you trust."

"If you tell, the bad person might hurt you," Stella said.

"If you tell a person you trust—like your mom and dad—they'll protect you," Willa said. What had prompted Stella to say this? How could Willa find out?

"Can we practice with the bandages now?" a girl asked.

"Yes. I want to be the patient," someone else shouted.

"I want to be the doctor," another girl said.

Willa had to let the moment pass. But she kept a close watch on Stella as the girls took turns fastening slings or trying out the flexible metal splints. Was the girl speaking from personal experience, or remembering things Olivia had told her?

She didn't have a chance to speak to Stella again before her time with this group was up. Willa spent the rest of the morning repeating the experience with younger groups of girls, finishing up with a class of six- and seven-year-olds who had a loud discussion about how awful shots were and the importance of washing your hands after you touched boys because of cooties.

The last session ended at twelve thirty and Mrs. Mason presented Willa with her own green Mountain Kingdom T-shirt and thanked her for coming. Willa headed back to her car. She was passing the mess hall when the back door opened and a small figure with a tail of brown hair darted out, then disappeared behind a tree.

Willa looked around. No one else appeared to have seen the girl, who she was sure was Stella. Moving cautiously, hiding behind trees as much as possible, Willa hurried after the girl, whose figure she could just make out ahead of her.

Willa ended up breaking into a run to keep up with

the swift little girl. She leaned against a tree and tried to catch her breath, watching as Stella tucked something in the crotch of a tree. She made sure her offering was secure, then turned and raced back toward camp.

And collided with a waiting Willa. The little girl looked up, wide-eyed, then burst into tears.

Willa knelt and patted Stella's shoulder. "It's okay," she said. "You're not in any trouble. I just wanted to make sure you were okay."

Stella continued to sob.

"What's wrong?" Willa asked. "What has you so upset?"

"My friend is hurt and lost and I'm so worried about her." The little girl leaned into Willa, sobs shaking her slight frame.

"Do you mean Olivia? Were you leaving something for her in the tree?"

"I put part of my lunch there." She looked up, expression pleading. "Please don't tell anyone. I'll get in trouble. Mr. Sprague caught me coming out here one day and I had to miss afternoon swimming as punishment. He said I was wasting food and that was wrong."

"Does Olivia come after you leave and get the food?" Willa asked.

"I don't know." Stella scrubbed at her wet eyes. "Sometimes when I come back the food is gone, but I don't know if Olivia gets it or an animal. I hope she gets it. I don't like to think about her hungry."

"Do you know where Olivia is hiding?" Willa asked.

"No. I promise I don't. If I knew, I would tell you. I'm worried about her."

"Do you know why Olivia ran away?" Willa asked.

Stella toyed with the friendship bracelet on her left wrist.

"She didn't tell me. And I didn't know she was going to run away, either. If I had, I would have told her not to."

"But she said something? Something to let you know she was upset?"

"She said she saw something she shouldn't have. And she said she was afraid."

"What was she afraid of?"

"She said if she told me I might get hurt, too."

Too. "Had someone hurt Olivia?" Willa asked.

"I don't know." Stella looked doubtful. "Maybe? I never saw her hurt. But then they found that shirt with her blood on it…" Her voice gave way to fresh sobs.

Willa waited for the sobs to subside. She searched for something to distract the girl. "Did you make your bracelet?" she asked. "It's pretty."

"Olivia made it." She held out her wrist, the show off the chevron pattern of pink, purple and green threads. "I made one for her." Fresh tears welled in her eyes. "A deputy showed me a bracelet they found in the mud. It looked like Olivia's. They wouldn't say, but I think maybe they found it with the shirt."

"How did you know about the shirt?" Willa asked. Surely no one had told the children.

"Mr. Sprague told me. The day he caught me with half my lunch wrapped in a napkin. He said I needed to stay close to camp or the person who had done that to Willa would hurt me the way they had hurt her."

She began to weep again. Willa held her tightly, and cursed Scott for frightening the child this way. "When did Olivia tell you these things?" she asked.

"The night before she left. The next day she seemed okay, and when I asked her how she was feeling, she said she was fine. But then, after dinner that night she was acting upset again. She didn't want to talk about it and told me not to worry, but how can I not worry when I don't even know where she is?"

Willa nodded. Olivia clearly needed help, but so did Stella. "When do you see your parents again?" she asked.

"Not for another month. When camp is over."

"Do you talk to them on the phone?"

"On Sunday afternoons. I told them last Sunday that I don't like it here anymore and I want to go home, but they said I had made a commitment and it was important that I keep it."

"Stella, look at me." Willa studied the girl's face. "Has anyone threatened to hurt you?"

She shook her head no.

"Has anyone done anything to make you uncomfortable?"

"No. Not how you mean."

"What other way is there?"

"I didn't like missing swimming that afternoon, but that was because I broke a rule. Not because anyone was bullying me. We studied about bullying in school, so I learned about that." She pushed away. "I need to get back to camp before somebody misses me. You won't tell anyone about the food, will you?"

"No, I won't. Not anyone at camp. I might tell another friend of mine, but he's very good at keeping secrets. And he'll make certain you don't get in any trouble. And wait just a second." She dug in her purse and pulled out a pen and a receipt. She turned the receipt over to the blank side. "What are your parents' names and their phone number?" she asked.

Stella's eyes widened. "You're going to call my parents?"

"Only if I need to. I might suggest they let you come home early, if that's okay with you."

Stella bit her lip, then nodded, and gave Willa the information. "Don't make it sound like I'm in trouble," she said.

"I won't. I promise."

Stella looked at Willa a long moment, then turned and raced away. Willa stood and walked to the fork of the tree. Half a dozen potato puffs, a corn dog and one broken cookie were wrapped in a napkin. Willa started to wrap the food again and return it to its hiding place when she saw the note in the corner of the napkin. Written in tiny letters, in pencil, was Stella's message to her friend: "Olivia, please come home."

I have to talk to you, but not at the sheriff's department, and not at my house.

Aaron stared at the message from Willa, heart racing, then replied, Did you learn something at the camp?

I'll tell you when we meet. Mount Wilson trailhead?

Why there? But he would find out when he saw her. He texted, I could be there at 3:30.

See you then.

He changed out of his uniform after his shift ended at three, and drove to the trailhead. Willa's Toyota was there, and she climbed out of the driver's seat when he pulled up beside her. She wore jeans and a lacy top, and carried a small pack.

"We don't have time to do the whole trail," she said. "But let's walk up to the first overlook."

"All right." He grabbed his own pack and followed her up. She was a strong hiker, with a confident stride. By the time the trail leveled out after the first half mile they were both breathing hard from the exertion. "What did you want to tell me?" he asked, unable to pretend patience any longer.

"Olivia's best friend at camp, Stella, was in my first class of the morning," Willa said. "She said some things that piqued my interest, but I didn't get a chance to ask many questions. Then I saw her right before I left and she had a lot of interesting things to say."

"Does she know where Olivia is now?" he asked. "Does she know why she ran away?"

"She doesn't know either of those things, but she said the night before she disappeared, Olivia told Stella she had 'seen something she shouldn't have,' and that she was afraid. Olivia wouldn't elaborate, and said she couldn't tell Stella anything else because she was afraid Stella might be hurt, *too.*"

"Had someone hurt Olivia?"

"Stella said Olivia didn't look hurt. But maybe it was something Stella couldn't see."

"Or maybe what Olivia saw was someone hurting someone else."

Willa started walking again. The trail was wider here, and Aaron fell into step beside her, matching his stride to hers. "Stella said she didn't know Olivia was planning to run away," she said. "When she found out Olivia was gone the next morning, she was really afraid."

"Why didn't she say anything to us when we questioned her?" Aaron asked. "Or to one of the counselors?"

"Because she was afraid," Willa said. "She didn't know

what Olivia had seen or who was involved so she kept her mouth shut. A pretty smart decision, considering."

Maybe it *was* smart, from a frightened child's point of view. "And she really doesn't have any idea where Olivia is now?"

"She says she doesn't and I believe her. She's really worried about her friend. She's been saving back part of her lunch every day and leaving it in a tree in the woods for Olivia."

"Does Olivia come to get it? Maybe we could hide and wait for her."

Willa shook her head. "Stella said sometimes when she comes back the food is gone, but she doesn't know if Olivia is taking it, or animals. I think it's probably animals. The tree where she's leaving the food is still in the camp. If Olivia is as frightened as Stella made her sound, I'm not sure she would risk coming that close."

"Does anyone else know about this?" Aaron asked.

"Stella said Scott caught her carrying part of her lunch outside the mess hall one day. He told her she needed to stay close to camp or the person who had hurt Olivia would hurt her. He told her about the bloody shirt they had found." She glared at Aaron. "What kind of person frightens a child that way?"

"One who wants her to stay close, no matter what," Aaron said. "What did he do then?"

"He made her stay in her cabin and miss afternoon swimming as a punishment for wasting food."

"He obviously didn't frighten her enough to make her stop leaving food for Olivia," Aaron said. "I still think it would be worth staking out that tree to see if Olivia shows up."

"If you do that, you can't tell anyone about Stella," Willa said. "I promised. And if someone at camp is the person who frightened Olivia away, I don't want to risk them going after Stella." They reached a small sign for the overlook and turned onto a short side trail. Thirty yards later the trail opened up to a view of the landscape below.

"I wanted to come up here and see this," Willa said.

Aaron moved in close beside her. Not touching, but close enough to smell her floral shampoo, and see the gentle rise and fall of her chest as she breathed. "I think Olivia is down there somewhere," she said.

"If she would come out of hiding, we could keep her safe," Aaron said.

"She must not believe that. Not yet."

"What could she have seen that has her so frightened?"

"Whatever it was, it was at the camp," Willa said. "You're going to have to dig deeper there."

He put a hand on her shoulder. She didn't pull away. "You need to tell all of this to the sheriff," he said.

"I promised Stella."

"Travis Walker is a good man. He's not going to endanger a child. But he needs to know about this. He's the only one who can authorize any kind of investigation at the camp."

She bowed her head. Her hair fell forward, revealing the nape of her neck, pale and vulnerable. As fragile as a child hiding food—and secrets—for her friend. Or another child, hiding in the wilderness. Or any human heart, so easily broken and difficult to mend.

"I'll talk to him," she said. "But only if you come with me."

"Of course." He put his arm around her and she leaned back against him. The position was so familiar, but he had never thought he would feel this closeness again. He didn't dare hope it would lead to anything else, but it meant a lot that she trusted him enough in this moment to lean on him, however briefly. Neither of them said anything for a long while, then she turned and walked back down the mountain, him following behind.

Chapter Thirteen

Willa had seen Sheriff Travis Walker around town, on search and rescue calls and during the search for Olivia. With leading-man good looks and a solemn, reserved demeanor, he had attracted the attention of more than one lovestruck tourist who had gone on to learn he was a happily married father of two. But it wasn't his looks or his attitude that intimidated Willa. As she sat across from him in his cluttered office at the sheriff's department, she was all too aware that he was a man with the power to put an innocent man—like her brother—behind bars. And the power to dismiss the concerns of someone like her.

"Aaron tells me you have some information that may help us in our search for Olivia Pryor," he said after Aaron had formally introduced them. Aaron sat in a second chair next to Willa, a silent, encouraging presence.

"I gave a first aid class at Mountain Kingdom Kids Camp this morning," Willa said. "The girls from Olivia's cabin were in my first class and one of the girls, Stella, told me Olivia confided in her that she—Olivia—had seen something she shouldn't have. She was clearly frightened, but she wouldn't tell Stella what she had seen or what had frightened her. She said she was afraid that Stella would be hurt, too. And the next night, Olivia ran away." Did summarizing the story this way made it sound trivial? "Stella was really afraid for Olivia. Whatever Olivia saw must have been bad. If we could find out what that was, maybe that would help us find a way to bring Olivia home safely."

"Tell me the timeline," Travis said. "When did Olivia see this event that upset her?"

"The night before she disappeared," Willa said.

"That would have been Saturday night," Aaron said. "The night of the bonfire."

The sheriff nodded. "Olivia was reported missing on Monday. We believe she ran away Sunday night."

Five days ago. For five days Olivia had been out there in the wilderness. Alone. Afraid. Hungry and thirsty. Cold.

"Stella has been leaving food for Olivia in a tree at the edge of camp," Willa said. "She doesn't know if Olivia is coming at night to take the food, or if animals are eating it. She swears she doesn't know where Olivia is now, and I believe her."

"We'll talk to her," Travis said.

Willa leaned forward. "Please be careful. Stella is terrified. She knows about the bloody shirt you found and she's afraid whoever hurt Olivia will come after her. I'm afraid of that, too. I think she needs to go home, away from the camp."

"We'll need to get in touch with her parents," Travis said. "Do you know their names?"

"I have their names and a phone number." Willa opened her purse and took out the receipt on which she had written the information and passed it across to Travis. "Try not to frighten her more. The poor girl is miserable, between worrying about her friend and being afraid."

Travis picked up the handset of his phone and punched in the number. "Mr. Ireland?" he asked. "This is Sheriff Travis

Walker in Eagle Mountain, Colorado… Your daughter is fine. I'm calling because we would like to talk to her about the disappearance of her friend Olivia, and we would like you and your wife present when we do so… Stella is not in any trouble. We understand she's very upset about her missing friend, and we believe she may know some small details that could help in our search for Olivia Pryor… It's very important that you bring her in as soon as possible… Tomorrow morning would be good. I know Stella will be happy to see you. One thing I have to ask is that you don't tell the camp or Stella ahead of time that you're coming. Simply show up and bring Stella here to the sheriff's department. We're on Second Street in Eagle Mountain… The camp might object, but they can't keep you from your daughter. If they give you any trouble, call me. I'm going to give you my direct number." He recited a phone number, then repeated it. "Thank you. I really appreciate your help."

He ended the call. "They're bringing her in tomorrow," he said.

"That was good, telling them not to contact the camp ahead of time," Willa said. "Will you tell them after the interview that Stella needs to go home with them? I'm afraid if someone at the camp did hurt Olivia, they might go after Stella, too."

"I'll tell them."

He thanked her again for coming in and she walked with Aaron to his truck. He had offered to drive her to the interview and she had gratefully accepted. "I don't want to go home yet," she said as he started the engine. "Gary is there and he'll ask about the interview. I'm not ready to talk about it yet."

"Where would you like to go?"

"Someplace quiet and private."

He considered this a moment, then shifted into gear and pulled out of the parking space. She didn't ask where they were going, merely stared out the window, her expression pensive.

AARON DROVE TO his house and pulled into the driveway. "Is this all right?" he asked as he shut off the engine.

Willa studied the A-frame, with its fading paint and ragged yard. It wasn't that different from her own rental. A comfortable place to stay, but not yet a home. "This is fine," she said, and got out of the truck.

She was waiting at the door when he came up behind her to open it. The living room was as she remembered from her visit three nights ago, cluttered and comfortable, dust motes drifting in the sunlight that arced through floor-to-ceiling front windows.

"I can make coffee," he said, shutting the door behind them. "Or tea."

"Let's just sit for a minute." She sat on the sofa. He started to take the chair across from her—the one she had chosen the other night—then shifted to sit beside her. Close, but not touching.

"Sorry the place is such a mess," he said, following her gaze to the shirt draped across the back of the chair and the empty glass on the coffee table.

"It's better than the place you were living in when we met," she said. "There were boxes everywhere."

"I had just moved and wasn't unpacked yet," he said. "It got better."

She angled toward him, smiling at the memory. "Do you remember the first time I saw it? The first time we went out?"

"The day we met. I remember."

She put a hand to her cheek, which felt hot. "I still can't believe how fast I fell for you. You brought in that prisoner to be stitched up and we started talking and the next thing I knew I was agreeing to have dinner with you. That night."

"I couldn't believe my luck," he said. "The minute I saw you I was just…bowled over. I knew I was completely monopolizing your time but I couldn't stop talking to you. I was sure you were going to think I was the biggest fool you had ever met."

"I didn't think that. I was just…mesmerized."

He laughed, from nerves as much as amusement. "No one has ever said that about me before."

"I don't know what it was about you," she said. "It was like…we had so much to say to each other. I didn't want you to leave, and I couldn't wait to see you again."

"When I asked you back to my place after dinner, I was sure you'd turn me down," he said. "I was already planning to ask to see you the next day. And I knew I'd call you the next morning, but you said yes."

"I had never done that before—gone back to a man's place when I'd known him less than twenty-four hours. Even as I was saying yes, I couldn't believe I was doing it." She fell silent, remembering what else she had done that evening—falling into bed with him as if they had known each other for months instead of hours. It was as if they had come down with a fever that left them only able to think about each other.

"That was a good night," he said. "A special night."

He slid his hand into hers and the warmth of him wrapped around her. That hadn't felt rushed or tawdry or any of the things she might have imagined sex with a man she scarcely knew would be. It just felt…right. She looked down at his hand. She would have denied she ever believed in love at first sight, but looking back, she could see she had started falling in love with Aaron during that first conversation, while she cleaned the cut hand of a bleeding prisoner and they talked about the phenomena of emergency rooms being busier during the full moon.

She closed her eyes against sudden tears, the pain of missing him overwhelming her. How had something so right ended so badly?

"Willa?" He stroked her hair, and turned her toward him. "What's wrong?"

She opened her eyes and looked at him, his features blurred but familiar—strong jaw, thick eyebrows, dark lashes any woman would envy. "I loved you so much," she blurted.

"I know."

His lips on hers were firm, not hesitant or doubting. *This is what I want,* the kiss said. And everything in her echoed, *This is what I want.*

She reached for him, sliding her fingers around the back of his neck to the warm, soft place beneath a tickling fringe of hair. She opened her mouth and more warmth flooded her as his tongue tangled with hers, every sensitive nerve alive to his touch. He slid his palm up to cup the side of her breast and she knelt on the sofa cushion beside him, then crawled into his lap, straddling him, hands gripping his shoulders while his fingers dug into the curve of her hips.

They began to undress each other, not talking. Not needing to talk. She pushed back his shirt and the cool metal of the St. Michael medallion brushed against her palm. He lifted his hips and she tugged off his jeans, then straightened so that he could pull her top over her head. She stripped off her jeans and underwear with no self-consciousness. She had been here before, with this man, and she had never felt safer.

Her fingers moved without her having to think, rediscovering territory that had once been as familiar to her as her own. His skin was firm and warm, taut over a muscular chest and arms. There was the mole on the left side of his ribs, and the perfect whorl of dark hair centered between his nipples. There was the lopsided indentation of his navel, and the small silvery white scar from the appendectomy he had had at age twelve. She pressed against him, and felt the rigid heat of his erection, and the answering flood of warmth within her.

He gripped her bottom and settled her more firmly against him, then kissed her long and hard until she was dizzy and breathless, trembling with need.

"Condom?" she asked, no longer capable of full sentences.

In answer, he gently shifted her off of him and stood, then took her hand and tugged her upright. She let him lead her down a hall to a bedroom—comforter pulled up over pillows, a single lamp casting a pool of light over the right side of the bed in the gloom of drawn curtains.

"I'll be right back," he said.

She lay back on the bed, the thrill of anticipation washing over her. She didn't allow herself to think—didn't give doubt time to take hold. Aaron returned in moments, a foil packet in his hand. The bed dipped as he lay beside her, and when he pulled her close she surrendered everything, no longer fighting what she had needed for so long.

AARON HAD DREAMED of making love to Willa again—tortured dreams after which he woke frustrated and grief stricken. There was no grief now, only the joy of knowing she was just as he remembered—just as beautiful. Just as passionate. Just as able to make him feel so much better than he deserved.

He wanted to take his time—to reacquaint himself with every inch of her. But neither of them could wait for that. When she whispered for him to hurry, the urgency in her voice sent a tremor through him. He unwrapped the condom and slid it on, then moved toward her. She moaned as they came together, and that was almost his undoing. Nothing had felt this right—ever. When he began to move, she moved with him, and smiled up at him, his own delight reflected in her eyes. Then she laughed, and he laughed, too, increasing the pace of their rhythm, wanting to memorize the incredible feel of her—of them together.

Then the intensity of the moment silenced them both, and they communicated only with a shifting of hips or the nudge of a hand. His heart pounded, and when he rested his palm between her breasts he felt the thud of her heart, too. Her face was flushed, her eyes glazed, and he knew she was close to the edge. He slid his hand down between them to touch her and felt her convulse around him, a tension that triggered his own release, powerful and overwhelming and humbling.

They lay together for a long while afterward, thin bars of white light showing around a gap in the curtains in the otherwise dim room. She rested her head in the hollow of his shoulder, one thigh draped over his thigh, her skin soft as satin, the perfume of her hair mixed with the musk of sex, taking him back to other bedrooms they had shared, as if scarcely a day had passed since they had last been together, instead of almost a year.

"I hope that wasn't a mistake," she said, breaking the silence.

"It wasn't a mistake," he said. The words hadn't alarmed him. He had known she would think this, even if she didn't say it. Willa had lost so much in her life she lived with the fear of loss even in the midst of bounty. He had tried to be that bounty for her. That he had failed still haunted him, but he was not one to dwell on the past. He could only look forward, and try to prove she had nothing to lose with him this time.

She shifted, and raised her head to look at him. "It can't be like before between us. I can't be that…consumed… again. I can't lose myself that way again."

"I never wanted you to lose yourself." He stroked her arm, the fine hairs soft against his fingers. "I don't want to own you or monopolize you or do anything but love you."

Her eyes met his, her gaze as open and honest as he had ever seen it.

"I'm scared," she stated.

"I know. I'm scared, too. Scared of screwing up. Scared of losing you again. But isn't it better to be scared together than apart?"

She lay down again, curled against him. "Yes," she said. "Yes, it's better."

He rested his hand on her back, and felt her relax and fall asleep. But he lay awake a long time. Being with her was better than anything else. But he didn't know if he could survive losing her again.

Chapter Fourteen

Saturday morning shortly before noon, Gage, Aaron, Jake and Ryker reported to the main office of Mountain Kingdom Kids Camp with a warrant to search the property. Other deputies waited outside for the order to begin combing through the various buildings on the property.

"Mr. Sprague isn't here," Mrs. Mason said. "I can't allow you to look at the files without his permission."

"We have a warrant, ma'am," Gage said. "We don't need his permission."

He stepped past and she watched, hands clutching a copy of the warrant, as the deputies filed into the office.

"What are you looking for?" she asked.

"Everything," Gage said. "It would be best if you waited in your office while we're here. We don't take any more of your time than necessary."

She pulled out a cell phone and punched in the number, listened for a moment, then hung up. "Mr. Sprague isn't answering his phone."

"Where is Mr. Sprague?" Ryker asked.

"I imagine he's where he always is these days," she said. "He's searching for Olivia Pryor. But I need him here. We've already had a set of parents show up and withdraw their child early from camp. I'm sure it's because of all the bad publicity about Olivia Pryor. But it's not our fault if one headstrong girl decides to run away."

Stella and her parents had met with the sheriff this morning at nine o'clock, and Stella's statement about Olivia seeing something that had frightened her, plus the sheriff's argument that it was possible Olivia was being held prisoner somewhere on the property, had resulted in a judge granting a warrant to search the camp once more—including the office, all outbuildings and the Sprague residence. These had been searched before, but with the cooperation of everyone involved. Camp employees and Scott himself had accompanied deputies as they searched for the missing girl. This time, they would also be looking for any evidence of a crime that might have involved Olivia, or that she might have witnessed.

They started with staff records. "We're looking for any kind of disciplinary action for inappropriate behavior with a child," Gage said. "Also any records of theft or vandalism. Maybe what Olivia saw was someone breaking the law."

The records search took very little time. With less than a dozen employees and very few records on them, going through all the files took less than an hour. "Everyone here is squeaky-clean," Ryker announced when they were done. "Either Scott has been very lucky with his hires or the records are lying."

Interviews with the staff revealed nothing, either. "We've got a really great bunch of people here," Wade Lawson told Aaron and Ryker. "Most of us have been here two or three summers, at least."

"You're telling me that all summer, nothing has turned up missing?" Ryker asked. "No one's gotten into any trouble at all?"

"The only trouble was when my brother died," Wade

said. "I still don't know what really happened that night, but I can't believe anyone here had anything to do with it. Everyone really liked Trevor."

"This is leading nowhere," Ryker said as he and Aaron walked back toward the lodge.

They detoured when Gage hailed them. The sergeant was coming out of Scott's house. "Find anything?" Ryker asked.

Gage shook his head. "The man lives like a minimalist. No photos, very few books, one file drawer full of personal papers. Nothing incriminating."

Aaron looked back at the log home, straight out of the 1970s, or '50s, or even '30s. "Didn't his family own this camp for years? Maybe his grandparents started it?"

"That's the story," Gage said. "But there's not one family heirloom in the place, unless you count a toaster that probably dates from the 1980s."

"Sarge!"

They turned to see Jake jogging toward them. He held out a small evidence bag. "Found this in Mrs. Mason's apartment."

Gage examined the plastic pouch, which contained a prescription bottle. "Seconal. The prescription is made out to Phyllis Mason."

"She said it was prescribed last year, when she was going through a difficult time. She didn't elaborate on what was wrong, but said she hadn't taken the pills in months."

Gage shook the bottle. "How many are in here?"

"Three. But she can't remember how many were left when she stopped taking them. She swears no one else has been in her apartment."

"Where is the apartment?" Gage asked.

"Upstairs, over the dining hall."

"Anything else of interest in there?" Gage asked.

"Nothing," Jake said. "I asked her if she knew Trevor Lawson. She said she had met him when he filled out the employee paperwork but she never spoke to him afterward. He had only worked part-time at the camp for about a month when he died."

"We'll see what we can get from this." Gage handed back the evidence pouch. "But lots of people have prescriptions for sleeping pills. It doesn't mean there's any connection to Trevor."

"Trevor died the night before Olivia disappeared," Aaron said. "Stella said Olivia was upset about something that happened the night before she ran away. Could she have seen something to do with Trevor Lawson's death?"

"Stella also said Olivia had been 'sad' for a couple of weeks before that," Ryker said. "I read that in one of her first interviews. I think that means whatever upset Olivia wasn't something new."

"All right, but what if she was sad about something— maybe homesick, something like that?" Aaron asked. "And then the night Trevor died, she saw something. Maybe she saw who killed him. That might have frightened her enough to run away."

"Trevor Lawson committed suicide," Gage said. "He drove his car off Dixon Pass."

"He was legally drunk and had Seconal in his system," Jake said. "But his brother swears Trevor didn't drink to excess or do drugs. And there were indications Trevor had been in a fight before he died."

"Maybe someone made sure Trevor wasn't in any shape to drive before he got into his car to go home that evening," Aaron said.

"They couldn't have been sure he would go off the road,"

Ryker said. "I've stopped plenty of drivers with blood alcohol levels higher than Trevor Lawson's who weren't showing any signs of being drunk."

"Still, what if Olivia saw something to do with Trevor's death?" Aaron said.

"You're going to have a hard time proving it," Gage said.

"Maybe. But if someone did do something to Trevor and they knew Olivia saw them, it would explain why she was frightened enough to run away."

"It could also explain the blood and the ripped shirt," Ryker said. "I can't help wondering if Olivia ever left this camp. There are a lot of places to hide a body around here."

"And we're searching them all," Gage said. "We've got a cadaver dog coming on loan from Mesa County tomorrow. Meanwhile, let's get back to work."

They trudged after him to take apart the storage shed and the kitchen, while workers huddled in the empty mess hall, casting hostile stares their way and muttering among themselves. No one liked disruptions to their routine, and everyone thought the deputies were wasting their time.

Aaron couldn't help thinking the same thing. They were missing something here. He had felt that way with other unsolved cases. If they could only discover the one missing piece of the puzzle, everything would shift into focus and they would find the guilty party. But all this searching wasn't turning up anything, and with a little girl's life at stake, they were running out of time.

GARY STOPPED BY the medical clinic a little after noon on Saturday. Willa spotted him coming in the door and rushed into the waiting room. "Gary! What are you doing here? Are you all right?" She searched him for any sign of injury or illness.

"I'm fine. The camp sent me home early."

"Why? What happened?"

He glanced around the empty waiting room. "The sheriff's deputies are at camp searching everything," he said, keeping his voice low. "From attic to basement. They came this morning with a warrant. Mrs. Mason was in a tizzy and Scott was nowhere in sight. He showed up two hours in and I thought he was going to stroke out, yelling at the cops to stop what they were doing. They went right on emptying drawers and going through files, as if they hadn't even heard him. About that time, Scott ordered all the kids confined to quarters and all nonessential personnel—meaning everyone but the counselors—to go home. He also told us not to talk to anyone, but I figure that's an order he can't really enforce."

The door buzzer sounded as a woman and a little boy entered.

Willa took Gary's arm. "Come back here where we can talk." She led him to the back of the building, and the small break room. "What are the deputies looking for?" she asked.

"They didn't say." He helped himself to a doughnut from a box someone had left on the counter. "You should ask Aaron. Maybe he'll tell you. He was there today. I saw him shifting boxes of canned goods in the storage shed. He didn't look too happy."

She turned away, praying she wasn't blushing. She couldn't claim she hated Aaron anymore, after the night they had spent together. But she wasn't ready to declare they were a couple again.

"Anyway, I stopped by to tell you a couple of the kitchen staff and I are going hiking along a stretch of the river near camp to see if we can find any sign of Olivia. We want to find her, but we don't want to find her, if you get what I mean."

She nodded. "You want to find her, but you don't want to find her body."

"Yeah. Anyway, don't wait up."

"You're a grown man, Gary. You don't have to check in with me."

"I don't have to, but if I don't, you'll worry."

"I can't help that."

He squeezed her shoulder. "I know. I hated it when I was a teenager and I'd come home and you'd be sitting there, waiting. But later on, I could admit it felt good, after Dad died, knowing I had someone looking out for me."

"We looked out after each other," she said.

"I was fifteen when Dad died. I could hardly look after myself, much less you. And I barely remember Mom. You were the one who washed my clothes and nagged me to clean my room and did all the mom stuff." He shook his head. "It's wild, when you think about it. You were only, what, nine or ten when she died? And I remember Dad was a mess for a while after that. You were the one who kept us together."

"Dad looked after us. I just did what I could to help." She still remembered the panicky feeling of coming home to an empty house, dust on the furniture and nothing waiting for dinner—as if her parents had simply walked out the door and forgotten to return. Forgotten they had two children to care for. She had done what she could to make sure Gary never had that feeling. And when their father had died when she was twenty, she had carried on looking after Gary. He was the only family she had left.

"Be careful," she said. "It's rough country out there."

"If it's rough for us, imagine what it's like for a little

girl. Let's hope she's a tough kid, like you were." He patted her back and left.

I wasn't tough, she wanted to tell him. *I just didn't know
what else to do.*

Maybe it was the same with Olivia. She had been fright-
ened and had run. Now she was just hanging on—for what,
Willa didn't know. She sent a silent message to the girl:
Keep fighting.

Aaron was waiting by Willa's car when she emerged from
the clinic that evening. He was exhausted from searching
through the Mountain Kingdom camp all day, his uniform
dirty from crawling through attics and moving aside boxes
in storerooms. He probably had spiderwebs in his hair. It
wasn't the most attractive picture to present a woman, but
if he had taken time to shower and change he would have
missed Willa. He wanted to see her, to reassure himself
she hadn't changed her mind about him after last night. He
didn't want to pressure her to spend more time with him
or to sleep with him again—though he would have welcomed both of those things. He just wanted to see her. To
know things were good between them again and that was
one less weight to carry.

"Aaron, you look awful," she said as she approached.
"Are you okay?"

"Just tired. I'll go home in a few minutes and take a
shower, I just wanted to make sure you were okay."

"Why wouldn't I be okay?"

"I was worried you were regretting last night." He
searched her face, trying to read her emotions. "I'm not,"
he added.

"No, I'm not regretting that." She moved closer, and
touched his shoulder. "You look exhausted. Gary told me

you were helping to search the camp. Did you find anything?"

"We didn't find Olivia, or any sign of her. I don't think we found anything else, either."

"I guess it's good that you didn't find her body, but how could she have simply disappeared?"

"It's easier than you might think, out here. Every few years a hiker goes missing. Some are never found."

"I've been learning about that in my search and rescue training. It's still hard to imagine." She took a step back. "Go home and rest. Maybe there will be better news tomorrow."

"I have to be back at the camp tonight. I was hoping you'd come with me."

"Why?"

"It's bonfire night. A camp tradition, every Saturday night."

"Is the public invited?"

"Not usually. But the sheriff told Scott he wanted to put some officers there to see if they could spot anything suspicious. Last Saturday was the night before Olivia went missing—the night when, according to Stella, she saw something that upset her. We're hoping we'll spot something to give us a clue what that something might have been."

"It was also the night Trevor Lawson died, wasn't it?" she asked.

"You made that connection, too?" He nodded. "Trevor was at the bonfire. He was supposedly fine then, but now I'm really curious to see what goes on at this thing, if it managed to upset two different people. Will you come with me to the bonfire?"

"Are you really supposed to take a date if you're working?"

"You'll be another set of eyes. And the kids like you."

"Did Scott agree to have a civilian there?"

"You'll be part of my cover. We agreed to come in plain-clothes so we don't upset the kids. The story is, Scott has invited some guests from town. He's done it before—usually parents or big donors."

"The campers have seen deputies at the camp all week," she said. "They're bound to recognize some of you."

"Probably. We'll do our best not to alarm them."

"All right. I'll come with you." She linked her arm with his. "I won't think of it as a date. I'll think of it as helping the police with their inquiries."

Chapter Fifteen

Willa and Aaron arrived at the camp just after sunset. The bonfire on the shore of the lake sent sparks into the sky, the wood snapping like twigs underfoot. They heard the buzz of conversation as they crossed the grass toward the shore, high children's voices soaring in the clear evening. The scent of woodsmoke perfumed the air, and a cool breeze raised goose bumps on Willa's bare arms, making her reach for the sweater she had brought.

"Did you go to camp when you were a kid?" Aaron asked.

"No."

"Did you want to?"

The memory came to her clearly—a summer when her two best friends were going to a sleep-away camp for two weeks. While she stayed home.

"One year I wanted to go," she said. "But it wasn't possible. I didn't even ask my dad."

"Because you knew he couldn't afford it?"

"I have no idea. But if I left, who would cook dinner for him and my brother, or do the laundry, or pack his lunch?" She shook her head. "Looking back, I can't believe I saw my father as so helpless. Surely he would have found a way to look after himself and Gary while I was away. But I took that on as my responsibility and I couldn't let it go."

"He let you take it on."

"He had a hard time after my mother died. It was probably easier to let me handle some of the things he didn't have the energy to do." She didn't want to think about that sad time, or about how things might have worked out differently. "What about you?" she asked. "Did you go to camp?"

"Boy Scouts. Camp Walla Walla or Winemuka or something like that. Two weeks of canoeing in deep water, archery with arrows with sharp points and dangerous crafts involving leather and sharp knives. All in the hands of preadolescent boys to which everything was a potential weapon. I'm amazed we all survived."

She laughed. "I think Mountain Kingdom is tamer than that. I didn't see a single sharp knife or arrow with a point in my visits here."

They reached the edge of the bonfire. A trio of girls were roasting marshmallows. Willa recognized Juliet, her purple cast covered with scrawled signatures.

"If you want a marshmallow, you have to ask Veronica," Juliet said. "She won't let you help yourself."

"Because some people take too many," a second girl, with black braids, said.

"Boys take too many," the third girl, a pixie-cut blonde, said, and all three dissolved into giggles.

Aaron touched Willa's shoulder. "I see someone I need to talk to," he said.

"Fine. I'm going to get a marshmallow."

He headed toward a cluster of cabins and she walked over to a folding table where Veronica sat, looking bored.

"Could I have a couple of marshmallows, please?" Willa asked.

Veronica handed her a bent coat hanger with two marshmallows impaled on the end. "I thought you were a nurse," she said. "Are you a cop, too? They told us there would be some cops here tonight."

"I'm friends with a cop." She glanced toward Aaron, who stood halfway between the bonfire and the cabins, talking with another counselor, a young man with wire-rimmed glasses.

Veronica followed her gaze. "Lucky you," she said. "He's hot. I noticed him yesterday, when they were searching the place."

"Did they find anything?"

"You tell me." She shrugged. "I don't think there's anything to find. This place is beyond dull. Olivia probably ran away because she was bored out of her mind."

"Were you her counselor?"

"One of them. And before you ask, I already told the cops she was normal as could be before she ran away. No tears. No moping."

"I heard she was sneaking out of her cabin for a while before she disappeared."

Her expression grew sullen. "I don't know anything about that. I'm not these kids' jailer. And I have to sleep sometime."

"If you had to guess, who do you think she was sneaking off to see? Did she have a boyfriend?"

"I never saw her so much as talking to a boy. Some of these girls, they're regular flirts. They hit on the male counselors, even—guys who are four and five years older."

"Did Olivia do that?"

"No. She was still a little girl. Which is a good thing, you know? She was kind of a tomboy. Athletic. Not afraid of spiders and stuff. She was having a lot of fun at camp. I don't know why she left."

A pair of boys approached, demanding marshmallows, and Veronica turned away.

Willa returned to the fire. She held her marshmallows over the blaze. Within seconds, one burst into flames. She blew it out, then popped it into her mouth—one side scorched, the interior half-melted, the other side cold and pillowy. Exactly as she remembered.

She roasted the other marshmallow and ate it, then looked around for something else to do. Aaron had disappeared, though she spotted a couple of other deputies, conspicuous by their alert attitudes and watchful gazes, despite their civilian clothing.

She scanned the crowd for anyone else she knew and her gaze came to rest on a girl who stood by herself on the edge of the firelight. The girl's stillness made Willa look more closely. She had the air of someone waiting for something—but not necessarily something good. She was tall and thin, growing too fast to have yet filled out, shiny brown hair hanging straight to the middle of her back. She wore a green Mountain Kingdom T-shirt and khaki shorts, and scuffed green sneakers. A boy ran up and said something to her, laughing. She scowled and slapped at him and he ran away, still laughing.

Then something caught the girl's attention from somewhere in the darkness. She looked away, then back, then darted off, disappearing quickly into the shadows.

Was she meeting someone? Another boy? Or had something else attracted her? Could it be Olivia, signaling a friend to meet her and bring food or a message or something else?

Heart pounding, Willa hurried after the girl. She had lost sight of her in the darkness, then she heard soft footsteps, moving toward one of the pit toilets. She slowed. Maybe that's all the girl had been doing—going to the restroom.

Unlike the other pit toilets, this one didn't have a light over the door. Why purposely choose one in the darkness? Willa stood next to a thick-trunked tree and waited. The door to the toilet didn't open, but the shadows to the side of the little building thickened as the girl stepped into them.

There was a scuffling sound. A sharp "no!" Willa started. There had been fear in that one word, and she felt an answering fear grip her throat.

She started to turn away—to go for help. Then another sound, like weeping. Willa still held the coat hanger she had used to roast the marshmallows. It wasn't much of a weapon, but it would have to do.

She rushed toward the pit toilet. "Hey!" she shouted. "What's going on back there?"

More scuffling, and one high-pitched scream. Footsteps raced away—someone young and light. The girl. Then strong arms grabbed Willa.

"What do you think you're doing?" a low voice growled, but before she could answer, a hand clamped over her mouth.

"Was it like this last week when your brother was here?" Aaron had spotted Wade Lawson and pulled him aside.

Wade glanced back at the bonfire—a five-foot wide, four-foot high blaze encircled by a double stack of rocks, the flames licking several feet into the night air. Kids crowded close, waving marshmallow sticks, talking, and laughing.

"Yeah. It's the same every week. Bonfire, kids, singing, marshmallows. Later one of the counselors will play guitar and lead a sing-along. Someone will tell a scary story. Then we've got scared kids hyped up on sugar that we have to take back to the cabins and try to settle down."

"About what time did Trevor leave?"

"Early. Maybe an hour in."

Aaron checked his watch. "It's seven o'clock. Did he leave before or after that?"

"About that, I guess. Maybe a little after? It was just getting dark. When the sun gets below the mountains, it gets dark fast."

"And you say he left here and headed for the pit toilet?"

"Yeah. That direction." Wade pointed to their left. "And I never saw him alive again. He was fine and definitely sober, yet you people tell me he got wasted, got in his car and drove off the pass. I can't even wrap my head around that." He grabbed at his hair. "It's like you're talking about somebody else."

"I'm sorry," Aaron said. "It must be tough being here, so soon after it happened."

"It sucks, but I don't have a choice. I've got a cabin full of kids to look after." He glanced over Aaron's shoulder. "I have to go. Malcolm! What did I tell you about burning holes in your shirt with that coat hanger?"

Aaron looked toward the row of pit toilets clustered under the trees. Three log-sided sheds, painted green, each with an LED light over the door.

Wait. There was a fourth. The light over this one was burned out. Something moved beside this one—a big shadow. A man-size shadow, struggling with something. Aaron started toward the scene, walking at first. Then he heard a scream and broke into a run.

WILLA GRABBED AT the hand clamped over her mouth and tried to pull it away. Whoever had hold of her was big. And strong. He jerked her off her feet and started dragging her, one arm clamped over her throat, cutting off her air. She continued to bat at him feebly, until he struck her with his fist. She reeled, vision blurring, but concentrated on keeping her wits about her. She remembered she had the coat hanger in her hand. With all the concentration she could muster, she gripped the coat hanger near the end, then waited until she felt the man's thigh against her leg. She reached back and plunged the wire end into his leg with as much force as she could muster.

The man swore, but not loudly, and kept his hold on her. But he loosened it enough she was able to slide down his body, out of his grip. He grabbed her shirt and she heard it rip as she lunged away from him. Then she was running, into the darkened woods, ducking and weaving and praying she wouldn't run over a cliff or into a tree.

AARON ALMOST COLLIDED with Scott as the camp owner staggered around the side of the pit toilet.

"Deputy!" he exclaimed, and clung to Aaron. "Did you see which way he ran?"

"Who?" Aaron helped Scott stand. The camp owner was red-faced and breathing hard, his hair disheveled.

"There was a girl. One of the campers. I saw her over here by the pit toilets. By herself. That's not safe. We tell the kids to always go to the pit toilets in pairs, especially at night. Then I realized she wasn't alone. Someone had hold of her. She was struggling. I ran up and yelled and the guy let her go and lunged for me. He stabbed me."

He looked down and Aaron saw the trickle of blood down Scott's thigh. He pulled out his radio. "We've got a bleeding man over here by the pit toilets near the bonfire," he said.

Jake responded that he would be right there, echoed by someone else.

Aaron stowed the radio. "What happened to the man who attacked you?" he asked.

"He ran off," Scott said.

"Which direction?" Jake asked.

"Up toward the lodge, I think."

Jake jogged up to them, Jamie close behind. "What's going on?" Jake asked.

Aaron gave them a quick recap of Scott's story. As he was talking, Scott interrupted, "Now that I'm thinking more clearly, I don't think the camper was a girl," he said. "It was a boy. A little boy. It can be hard to tell when they're little, but I'm sure now it was a boy."

"What happened to the boy?" Jamie asked.

"He ran off," Scott said.

"Which direction did he go?" Jake asked.

Scott looked around. "I'm not sure. Back toward the bonfire?"

"Do you know the boy's name?" Jamie asked. "Which cabin he's in?"

"I'm sorry, I don't. It all happened so fast." Scott put a hand to his head. "I'm not feeling so well." He carefully lowered himself to the ground and buried his face in his hands.

"The ambulance should be here soon," Jamie said.

"I don't need an ambulance." Scott looked up. "I just need to rest a moment and I'll be fine."

"The paramedics are on their way," Jamie said. "You can let them check you out."

"I'm going to look for the guy who stabbed him," Aaron said, and headed toward the lodge, leaving them to deal with Scott.

The grounds of the camp were deserted, with all the campers and staff at the bonfire. Aaron slowed to a jog, then a walk. The lodge was bathed in floodlights, but he didn't see anyone up there. Scott's attacker could be hiding in the shadows.

Aaron thought better of running into trouble and keyed the mic again. "I'm up here at the lodge, where Scott said his assailant headed," he said. "I don't see anyone, but it might be a good idea to get a few people up here."

"We're headed your way," Gage replied.

Aaron settled in the shadow of a tree, where he hoped he would be invisible to anyone watching. After a moment he keyed the mic again. "Scott said something about one of the campers who ran away. Someone should look for him—or her, Scott seemed confused on that point—and make sure they're okay."

"Jamie's already on it," Gage said. "Sit tight until we get to you."

He leaned against the tree and stared up at the lodge. He hoped someone would tell Willa what was going on. He would text her when he got the chance, but didn't want to light up his phone, in case someone was watching. She would be all right, he told himself. She had always been good at looking after herself.

Chapter Sixteen

Willa ran until her sides ached. As her eyes adjusted to the darkness she could make out more of the terrain, bathed in the glow of a moon that was three-quarters full. She pressed up against the fat trunk of a ponderosa pine and waited for her breathing to slow, listening for the sounds of footsteps following her.

She could no longer see the lights from the camp, or hear the children singing or any sound but the pounding of her own pulse and her still-ragged breathing. Not so much as a bird disturbed the darkness, which felt thick and black, despite the moonlight. She had lost her bearings in her flight, and wasn't even sure which direction she needed to go to get back to the camp. She reached for her phone, but couldn't find it. She checked every pocket, then realized it must have fallen out, either while she was running, or during her struggle with her attacker.

Her attacker. Who was he? She had the impression of bulk, and strength, but it had been impossible to see him in the dark, and he had held her from behind. Was it the same man who had attacked Olivia? Renewed fear gripped her at the idea. The man who had held her had meant to hurt her; she was sure. Had they all been wrong from the beginning of the search in thinking that Olivia was still alive, either lost or deliberately hiding in the wilderness? Had she died that first night, her body hidden where they would never find her?

He had been trying to hurt another camper when Willa had interrupted him. She had to get back to camp and tell Aaron and the others so that they could stop him. She looked around her, but could make out little in the nighttime gloom. Even though her eyes had adjusted to the dimness, and moonlight outlined the trunks of trees closest to her, nothing looked familiar. Which way was the camp?

She tried to remember what her fellow search and rescue team members had said about navigating in the wilderness. But the only lesson she had had so far was in using a compass and noticing landmarks. Then there was the standard advice to stay put if you were lost. But was that a good idea when someone might be coming after you? She didn't think she had wounded her attacker very seriously. He was bound to be furious, and determined to get even.

She started walking in the direction she thought would lead her toward the camp. The trick would be finding Aaron or another deputy before her attacker found her.

She hadn't gone far before something caught at her foot and she fell, hard. She cried out as she hit the ground, and rolled onto her side, gasping. After a moment, the pain subsided and she sat up. She tried to stand, but pain shot through her and her leg gave way. She sat down, waiting until the throbbing subsided, then gingerly ran her hands down her leg to her ankle. She was able to squeeze it, then rotate it gently. Not a break. Just a slight sprain.

She tried again to stand, gritting her teeth, and this time was able to remain upright. But she wasn't going to go far or very fast like this.

Then her heart slammed against her ribs as she heard

footsteps approaching. She bit her lip to keep from crying out, and tried to gauge where the sound was coming from. Ahead of her, and to the right. If she stood very still, maybe whoever it was would pass her by.

"Don't be afraid," a soft voice said. "I'm not going to hurt you."

A slight figure emerged from the shadows—a girl with a backpack, a stout walking stick in one hand. Her face was dirty, her jeans with a rip in one leg, but she looked healthy.

"My name is Olivia," she said. "Have you been looking for me?"

HANNAH GWYNN WAS one of the paramedics who responded to the call for assistance at the camp. She and her partner, a reedy young man named Henry, met Deputy Declan Owen in the camp's parking lot and hiked to the scene by the pit toilets, where Scott remained sitting on the ground. But at the sight of the paramedics, he tried to struggle to his feet.

"Remain still, Mr. Sprague," Jamie urged. "Let them examine your leg."

"I can't leave the camp while there's someone here who's attacked one of my campers," Scott said, though he remained sitting.

"Can you describe the attacker?" Jake asked.

"I didn't see much in the dark. It was a man. Big. And he stabbed me."

Hannah knelt beside Scott and directed the beam of a flashlight at his thigh. "It looks like the bleeding has stopped," she said. "I'm going to need to cut away your pants to get a better look." Before he could protest, she started cutting the cloth where a rusty streak of blood trailed down the khaki fabric. "It looks like a puncture wound," she said when the injured area was exposed. "Not a knife. Something small. Maybe an ice pick? Or a pen?"

Jake emerged from the other side of the pit toilet. "I found this behind the outhouse," he said, holding up something in a gloved hand. "I think it has blood on it."

He moved closer and they studied the item he held. "It's a bent coat hanger," Jamie said. "The kind the kids are using to roast marshmallows."

"Were you attacked by one of the campers?" Jake asked.

"Of course not." Even in this dim light, they could see his face redden. He was a big man. Even armed with a coat hanger, a child wouldn't have much of a chance at overcoming him.

"I'm going to look for the camper who was supposedly being attacked," Jamie said, and set off toward the camp.

Jake leaned forward to take a closer look at Scott's face. "Are those scratches on your cheek?" he asked.

Scott put a hand to his face. "I must have scraped it on a branch. We need to have the trees trimmed. Those low-hanging branches are a hazard in the dark." He winced as Hannah flushed the wound on his thigh with saline.

"I don't think you're going to need stitches, Mr. Sprague," Hannah said. "Are you up to date on your tetanus vaccine?"

"Yes," he said. He shoved to his feet. "I'll be fine."

"You need to be careful of infection," Hannah said.

"I promise I'll put some antibiotic ointment on it when I get to my office." He looked down at his torn trousers. "I need to change."

"Are you sure you don't have any other injuries?" Hannah said. "Let me check your blood pressure. You look very pale."

"I'm fine," Scott said with more force. Then more weakly

he continued, "Thank you for your concern, but I really need to take care of my campers."

"No," Jake said. "You need to come to your office with us."

"I don't have time for that now," Scott said. "And you need to find the man who attacked that child and injured me."

"We're looking for the camper. In the meantime, we need you to answer some questions."

"I've already answered your questions. Over and over again," Scott said. "None of them are helping you find Olivia. Or stop people like this man who attacked me."

"We have some different questions now," Jake said. He took Scott's arm as Declan moved in on the other side. "These are about what really happened here tonight."

AARON, GAGE and two other deputies searched all around the lodge and found no one.

"It doesn't even feel like anyone has been here," Gage said when they reconvened in front of the lodge. His phone beeped and he pulled it out, "It's Jake," he said, after glancing at the screen. "Yeah?" he answered. He listened for a moment, then ended the call. "I have to go," he said. "The rest of you, get back to the bonfire. You're looking for an upset kid who may or may not have been attacked by the pit toilets an hour or so ago."

"The kid Scott saved?" Aaron asked.

"Supposedly," Gage said. "We need to talk to them and find out what really happened."

Aaron pulled out his phone and texted Willa:

Sorry I went awol. Something came up. Headed back to the bonfire now.

She didn't answer, but who knew if she could even hear her phone, with all the noise around the fire now. Someone was leading a sing-along, complete with shouted choruses and fits of laughter. He circled the firepit, alert for Willa's blond hair or the pink of the sweater she had been wearing.

Halfway around, he met Shane, who was also searching. "Have you seen Willa?" Aaron asked him.

"No. I'm looking for one of the campers. Tall, thin, long brown hair. Her name is Kelli, one of the older girls. Another girl said she saw her headed toward the pit toilets right before all the commotion with Scott."

"I thought Scott said it was a little kid he rescued—a little boy," Aaron said.

Shane shrugged. "I don't know about that. But if this girl was near the pit toilets about the time the attack happened, she might have seen something."

"Okay. I'll look for her, too." He had an uneasy feeling in his stomach. Maybe Willa had gotten angry that he had ditched her and decided to go home. She could have called Gary to pick her up, or caught a ride with someone else. He tried texting her again.

Sorry I was such a bad date. We thought we had something.

He stared at the screen, willing her to answer. But there was no reply.

"Have you two seen anything?"

He turned to see Jamie walking toward him. "I found another girl who said she saw Kelli running toward her cabin about half an hour ago," Jamie said. "She said Kelli looked really upset."

"Which cabin?" Shane asked.

"Pine Cabin—the same cabin Olivia was in. Can one of you come with me to talk to her?"

"I'll go," Aaron said. Anything to distract him from worrying about Willa.

He followed Jamie across the campground. "There are a lot of dark hiding places out here in the woods," Jamie said. "I'm thinking a girl wouldn't venture out here alone unless she was really upset about something."

"Being attacked by a stranger would qualify as upsetting," Aaron agreed.

Light shone through the front windows of the cabin, a rectangular log structure with green shutters. They knocked on the door. After a moment, the door eased open and a slender girl with long brown hair looked out. Her eyes widened when she saw Jamie and Aaron.

"Did you catch him?" she blurted.

"Catch who?" Aaron asked.

"You two are cops, right?"

"We are," Jamie said. "Can we come in and talk to you for a minute? I'm Jamie and this is Aaron. Are you Kelli?"

She looked past them. "There's no one else with you, is there?"

"No," Jamie said.

The girl held the door open wider and stepped back to let them pass. She moved over to a bunk and sat on the edge of the mattress. "Where's Mr. Sprague?" she asked.

"Mr. Sprague is with some other deputies," Jamie said.

Kelli gnawed at her thumbnail. "Are they, like, arresting him?"

"Do you think we need to?" Jamie asked, her voice gentle.

Kelli burst into tears. Jamie moved to her side. Kelli leaned into her, sobbing. Jamie patted her back.

"If Scott has done something to hurt you or anyone else, we will arrest him," she said. "You don't have to worry about him hurting you again."

Aaron sat opposite on another bunk, feeling helpless in the face of this child's obvious pain.

"Aaron, could you get us some tissues?" Jamie asked.

He found a box of tissues on a table by the door and brought them to her. Kelli pulled out several and blew her nose.

"When you're ready, could you tell us what happened?" Jamie asked.

"Yes." Kelli's voice was stronger than Aaron had expected, tinged with anger. She blotted her eyes and raised her head. "I want to tell you what happened. I want him to get everything he deserves."

"We want that, too," Jamie said.

"Mr. Sprague is a creep and a perv," Kelli said. "He pretends to be all concerned about us campers but really he's just waiting for a chance to grope one of us. I even fell for his nice act, then, a couple of days ago, he cornered me on the way back from evening assembly. He said he needed help with something in his office. The next thing he had me in there and he was trying to feel me up and stuff."

"That must have been terrifying," Jamie said.

"It was." She looked at Jamie with pleading eyes. "At first I was just, too grossed out to even move. Then I kind of woke up and tried to fight him off, but he said no one would hear me. There isn't anybody in that part of camp at that time of evening. Everyone is back here at the cabins, getting ready for bed."

Fresh tears welled in her eyes. Aaron fought down a rage that squeezed his chest.

"Did Mr. Sprague threaten you if you told anyone?" Jamie asked.

Kelli nodded. "Yes. And not just me." She bowed her head, her fingers shredding the tissue. "I have a little sister. She's eight. She's in Willow Cabin. Mr. Sprague said if I didn't do what he wanted—everything he wanted—he would hurt her." She began to sob again.

Jamie's expression remained neutral, but Aaron sensed the anger radiating off of her. "Thank you for telling us," she said. "I know it's not something that's easy to talk about. What happened tonight?"

Kelli sniffed and blotted her eyes. "He sent me a message this afternoon. He said I needed to wait by the bonfire and when he signaled, I was to meet him by the pit toilets— the one with the burned-out light. I didn't want to do it, but I didn't have a choice. I couldn't let him hurt Emma."

Jamie handed her more tissue and waited until once more her tears subsided. She looked at Aaron. "You'd better notify Gage."

Aaron moved toward the door to step outside to make the call, but before he could open it someone knocked.

Declan stood on the top step, a plastic bag in one hand. "I found this on the ground by the pit toilet," he said. "It might be the girl's phone. It keeps buzzing, but I couldn't figure out how to unlock it."

Aaron stared at the phone. Flowered case, with a purple stick-on socket on the back. "That looks like Willa's phone," he said.

"What would Willa's phone be doing behind the pit toilet?" Declan asked.

Aaron took out his phone and punched in Willa's number. The phone in the bag vibrated.

He took the bag and turned back to Kelli and Jamie.

Even though he knew the answer, he asked Kelli, "Is this your phone?"

She looked at the phone in the bag. "No."

He kept his voice even. "Was there anyone else there at the pit toilets tonight, when you went to meet Mr. Sprague?" he asked.

"No." She wet her lips. "I mean, not at first. He was waiting for me and he…he tried to kiss me. I tried not to struggle, but he was holding me so tightly, he was hurting me. I cried out, and I scratched at his face. He didn't like that. He slapped me. And then someone shouted at us."

"Who shouted at you?" Aaron asked.

"A woman. I didn't get a very good look at her. She had blond hair, and she ran toward us. Mr. Sprague let me go and I ran. I ran all the way back here." She looked at Jamie. "Did I do something wrong?"

"No. Of course not." Jamie patted her hand and sent Aaron a questioning look.

"I'm sure this is Willa's phone," he said. "I think she was the blonde woman who shouted at Mr. Sprague."

"Willa is the nurse who gave the first aid class to campers yesterday," Jamie said. "Do you think this woman was her?"

"I don't know," Kelli said. "It was dark and I didn't get a good look. I just wanted to get away."

"I've been searching for Willa and I can't find her," Aaron said. "After Kelli left, Scott would have attacked her. He would have wanted to stop her from telling anyone what she had seen."

Aaron was a cop. He had been in scary situations before. Once a burglar had held a razor to his throat, the sharp blade nicking him and drawing blood. He had talked down drunks armed with broken beer bottles, and done traffic stops with semitrucks whizzing by inches from his back. But never had fear hit him the way it did now—clutching his throat and threatening to pull him under.

Jamie studied him, then pulled out her radio. "We need to talk to Gage," she said. "And we need to talk to Scott."

Chapter Seventeen

"You have to bend down kind of low to get in here, but I promise it's all right." Olivia put her hand on top of Willa's head and urged her to crouch down farther to squeeze into a narrow opening between two boulders. Willa did so, crawling on hands and knees through a short passage, gravel digging into her knees. Just when she was sure she couldn't go any farther—the opening was too narrow—she felt fresh air against her face, and popped out into a wider space.

Olivia scooted in after her. She took something from her pack, then switched on a little LED light and set it on a tree stump. Willa looked around at a circular space, about four feet across with a floor of smooth sand. She raised her eyes to the ceiling, dark and flat. "That's a tarp up there," Oliva said. "I stole it from a wood pile at camp. I don't think anyone has even missed it yet. The outside has about a foot of leaves over it. You'd have to dig down to even see it. It took me most of a day to construct it, but once I had it in place I didn't have to keep moving."

There was no missing the pride in the girl's voice.

"I'm impressed," Willa said truthfully. "Did you make the brush shelter in the national forest, too?"

"I did. But I only spent one night there before a hiker found it. I left to take a look around and when I came back,

I saw a woman nosing around. I knew I had to have some-place better. Someplace closer to camp, so I could keep track of what was going on." She knelt and opened her pack again. "Would you like some tea? I have a little stove and I can heat water. I only have one cup but we can share."

"Tea would be good." Willa sat with her back against the wall, knees bent, and watched the girl unpack a sin-gle-burner stove, like the kind used by backpackers. Olivia turned the knob and hit a striker and the stove lit. Then she filled a small metal cup from a bottle stowed in the side of the pack and set it over the flame to heat. She took a bag with what looked like shredded leaves in it and carefully sprinkled some in the cup. She looked up and caught Willa watching her.

"It's just dried mint and some clover. It tastes better than you might think." Olivia sat back and they waited for the water to boil. "How's your ankle?" she asked after a moment.

Willa had forgotten all about her ankle. She felt it. Only a little puffy. "Not bad."

"Did you hit your face when you fell?" Olivia asked. "Your lip is all swollen, and I think you're going to have a black eye."

Willa touched the corner of her mouth and winced. She patted the puffiness around her eye. "Someone attacked me," she said. "By the pit toilet. He was… I think he was molesting a girl. One of the campers. I yelled at him and he let her go and went after me."

"Oh God." Olivia buried her face in her hands, and her shoulders began to shake.

Alarmed, Willa crawled to her. "What's wrong? What did I say?"

Olivia raised her head and wiped at her eyes. Then she

leaned forward and switched off the burner. "That will need to steep a minute." The only sign that she was still upset was the way her hand trembled as she pulled it away from the stove. She took a deep breath and looked at Willa. "I'll bet it was Scott Sprague who hit you. He hit me, too. But he killed Trevor. Or, I'm pretty sure that's what he was doing when I saw him. That was why I had to run away. As long as he's still walking around free I can't go back."

"Mr. Sprague killed Trevor Lawson?" Willa asked.

Olivia nodded. "I think so."

"But why?" Willa asked.

"Because Trevor interrupted Mr. Sprague when he was feeling me up behind the pit toilet, just like you interrupted him today. It was what Mr. Sprague did. He took girls back there on bonfire nights—and other times, too—and kissed you and fondled you and…and other things. If you cried too loud or threatened to tell, he would hurt you even more. He said if I told anyone what he did he would say I lied and no one would believe him. He said he had done the same thing before. I knew he was telling the truth because I had heard that the year before some girl accused him of molesting her and he called her a liar with a sex addiction and her parents believed him and not her. I figured the same thing would happen to me. Everyone knew I had been sent to camp because I was seeing an older boy. But the thing is, Jared and I never actually had sex. Nobody believed that, either."

She leaned forward and picked up the cup and passed it to Willa. "It should be ready now. Sorry, you kind of have to strain out the leaves with your teeth."

Willa tested the tea, more out of politeness than anything else. "It's not bad," she said.

"It would be better if I had sugar, but I forgot to take

any of that. I have a couple of cookies, though." She dug in her bag and pulled out a bundle wrapped in plastic. "Stella left them for me a couple of days ago. She didn't know I was the one taking the food she left but she really helped me out. She didn't leave anything today, though. I hope she didn't get in trouble."

"You eat the cookies," Willa said when Olivia offered her one. "I ate at the bonfire."

"Smores!" Olivea groaned. "What I wouldn't give for one of those."

Willa set aside the tea. "How did you learn to do all of these things?" she asked. "The shelter and the tea and everything."

"From books, mostly. I like to read adventure stories. And some of the stuff I just figured out on my own." She popped a piece of cookie into her mouth and chewed, then swallowed.

"Did you make the trap in the woods?" Willa asked. "The pit with the branches over it?"

"You know about that?" She rose up on her knees, her expression excited. "I made that after I saw Mr. Sprague sneaking around the woods, looking for me. I was really hoping he'd end up in that hole, unable to get out, and nobody around to hear him yell. Too bad it didn't work."

"Someone else fell into it," Willa said. "A man who was searching for you. He broke his leg and a couple of ribs."

Olivia looked stricken. "Oh no!" She flapped her hands. "That wasn't supposed to happen! I didn't think anyone else would be out there. Oh gosh, I'm so sorry. Is he going to be okay?"

"He'll be okay. But why would you make a trap like that?"

"I just saw the hole and thought it would be perfect." She

groaned. "I really only wanted to get back at Mr. Sprague. I didn't think about anything else. What happened to the trap?"

"Sheriff's deputies marked it so no one else will fall in."

"Good."

"Are there any other traps in the woods we should know about?" Willa asked.

"None, I promise."

"How about other shelters or hiding places?"

"None of those, either. Once I fixed up this place, I didn't need anything else." She sighed. "It was almost fun, at first, figuring things out and building stuff. But it's getting old."

"So many people were searching for you," Willa said. "How did you keep from being found?"

"It wasn't as hard as you might think. Big groups of people in the woods make a lot of noise. Most of the time I could hear them coming from a long way away. I doubled back behind them and hid in places they had already looked." She frowned. "The dogs were harder to avoid. I did a lot of things like walking in streams or across rocky places. I climbed trees and walked along fence rails. It was kind of a game. I think they did pick up my scent a few times, but they always lost it. As miserable as the rain was, I think it helped destroy my scent."

She rested her chin on her upraised knees. "I saw Mr. Sprague looking for me a couple of times. He was alone, sneaking around. He was right by one of my hiding places one time and I thought I would die before he finally left— I was so scared. I knew if he found me, he would kill me." She lowered her voice to a deep, nasal timbre, not unlike the camp owner's. "Poor little Olivia, she had an accident in the woods. Isn't it terrible?"

"I'm glad you're okay," Willa said. She hesitated, then

added, "Do you mind telling me what happened with Trevor?"

"I don't mind. I planned all along to tell someone, as soon as I was sure I was safe from Mr. Sprague." She sat back, considering. "Last week, at the bonfire, Trevor came around the corner of the outhouse and his flashlight lit up the whole scene—gross Mr. Sprague leaning over me, trying to stick his tongue down my throat, him with his pants already undone. I screamed and Mr. Sprague turned around. I ran away, but then I had to stop and look back. I was hoping to see Mr. Sprague on the ground, being beaten to a pulp by Trevor, who wasn't a really big guy, but he wasn't little, either, and he was a lot younger and stronger than Mr. Sprague. Instead, I saw Mr. Sprague punch Trevor, and Trevor went down like a fallen tree. Then Mr. Sprague dragged him over to this cabin nobody uses anymore. A night watchman used to use it, I guess, though now the kids just make up stories about how the watchman hanged himself there and the place is haunted. That didn't really happen, did it?"

Willa shook her head. She had no idea, but she didn't want to interrupt the flow of Olivia's story. The girl finished her cookie and picked crumbs off her lap. "After Mr. Sprague hauled Trevor to the cabin, I sneaked up and watched through the window. He'd switched on one of those LED lights we all carry around, like this one." She nodded to the light on the ground between them. "Mr. Sprague tied Trevor to a chair, then left for a little bit. He locked the door behind him. I tried to break the lock but I couldn't, and I had to run hide again when I heard Sprague coming back. Trevor was awake by that time, and throwing himself around, trying to break free. Mr. Sprague pulled out a really big pistol and put it to Trevor's head. I thought I was going to die right there. If he had shot Trevor, I might have—not died, maybe, but I bet I would have passed out. Instead, Sprague handed Trevor this big bottle of whiskey and made him drink it. He held the gun there until Trevor had drained about half of it. Then Mr. Sprague pulled his head back and forced something down his throat. Maybe pills or poison or something. Then he made Trevor drink some more."

She bowed her head and fell silent. Willa waited a moment, then prompted, "What happened next?"

Olivia blew out a breath. "I stayed there watching a really long time, until Mr. Sprague untied Trevor and led him to the parking lot and helped him into his car. I thought everything would be all right then. He was letting Trevor go. So I sneaked back to my cabin and went to sleep."

"And the next day you found out Trevor had died?"

She nodded. "Yeah. I saw his brother, Wade, out by the boat house. I could tell he'd been crying. I asked him what was wrong and he told me about his brother. I wanted so bad to tell him Trevor didn't commit suicide—that Mr. Sprague had gotten him drunk and poisoned him. But then Mrs. Mason came up and told me I needed to get back to my cabin. Everybody knows she's Mr. Sprague's stooge, so I couldn't say anything with her standing there."

"What do you mean, Mrs. Mason is Mr. Sprague's stooge?"

"Oh, she's got this huge crush on him. You can tell by the way she moons over him. She does anything he tells her, and she's always spying on us and reporting back to him, even though he either ignores her or orders her around like his personal servant. But if any little rule gets broken, he'll end up hearing about it, and we know she's the one telling him. I'd feel sorry for her if it wasn't so gross."

"Why did you have to run away?" Willa asked.

"Because Mr. Sprague sent me a note to meet him Sunday night. He did that sometimes. I had to sneak out and go or something horrible would happen. I know it wasn't smart or brave of me or anything, but that man scares me. So I went and let him do his nasty thing and kept my mouth shut. I figured camp would be over in a few weeks and I'd never have to see him again."

She fiddled with her shoelaces. Willa wanted to reach out and pull her close, to tell the girl that none of this was her fault. But would those words from a stranger mean anything?

Olivia looked at Willa again, determination in her eyes. "When I got word that Mr. Sprague wanted to see me that night, I was terrified. I figured he would kill me, the way he killed Trevor. He knew I could tell everyone he was the last person who had been with Trevor, even if he didn't know I had seen what he had done in that cabin. It would be a lot harder for him to make people believe I was lying about something like that."

"So you decided to leave instead?"

"Yeah. I took what food I could from dinner and stuffed it in my pockets, then took an extra blanket and some water and camped out in the woods. The next day I decided I could do better and took a sleeping bag and a pack and more food from the shed. I had to break into the building but it wasn't that hard. That door is really old and kind of flimsy."

"They found a shirt," Willa said. "With your blood on it."

"Oh yeah, that." Olivia made a face. "I really wanted the cops to take a good look at Mr. Sprague. I knew I wasn't the first girl he had bothered, so I thought if they started asking questions, someone would say something. So I took one of my old shirts and ripped it up and put that blood on it."

"You put your own blood on it?" Willa couldn't keep the horror from her voice.

"Gross, right? But we had a first aid class and I remembered one of the things they said was that head wounds bleed a lot, even if they're not serious. So I stabbed my forehead with a pair of scissors." She pointed to an inch-wide cut on her forehead, already almost healed over. "It hurt so bad! And I felt pretty stupid. But it did bleed a lot, and I wiped it all up with that shirt and shoved it under the edge of Mr. Sprague's house. It was raining so hard I just hoped the rain wouldn't wash all the blood away before someone found it. But then they did find it and they didn't even look at Sprague."

"So many people were searching for you," Willa said. "Why didn't you go to one of them and tell them what happened?"

"Because I figured the first thing they would do is take me back to camp, where Mr. Sprague would make a big deal about me being a runaway juvenile delinquent who made up lies because I didn't want to get in trouble. And then when all the cops left he would strangle me in my sleep or something."

"They're going to be looking for me now," Willa said. Aaron would be looking for her. He would know she wouldn't leave without an explanation.

"I know." She picked at the frayed hem of her jeans. "But they'll believe you. You're an adult. So then maybe they'll believe me, too."

"They'll believe you," Willa said. She slid over until she was next to the girl and put her arm around her. Olivia had done a good job of surviving on her own, but for all her maturity, she was still a little girl.

She laid her head on Willa's shoulder. After a while, she

said, "It was fun at first, hiding from everyone, making this hiding place and stealing food. But I'm really tired now, and I think I'm ready to go home."

"Do you know how to get back to the camp from here?"

"Yes. But we need to wait until morning. Trying to get anywhere in the dark is dangerous. I fell into a gully one evening and it took me hours to climb out."

"Promise you'll go with me back to the camp in the morning," Willa said.

"I promise." She yawned. "If I spread out my sleeping bag, we can both sleep on it. It's better than the hard ground. And I have the blanket from my bunk."

They made their bed and Olivia turned out the little lantern. Soon she was sleeping, breathing evenly next to Willa. But Willa lay awake, staring into the darkness, praying for morning to come soon.

KELLI AGREED TO come with Aaron and Jamie to speak with Gage. "I figure I'm safer with you guys than here in this cabin by myself," Kelli said.

"We won't leave you alone until we're certain you're okay," Jamie said. "But Sergeant Walker needs to hear your story so we can take Mr. Sprague into custody. Aaron and I can tell him what you said, but it will be better if he hears it from you. And he may have more questions for you."

"I can talk to him." She stood, then hesitated. "Can I make sure Emma is okay, first? I mean, what if Mr. Sprague was so mad after I ran away that he went after her?" All color drained from her face and Jamie reached to steady her. "I just now thought of that."

"I'll find Emma," Declan said. "Do you know where she is?"

"If the bonfire is still going, she'll be with the younger

girls. Their counselor is a woman named Sage. Or they'll all be in Willow Cabin. It's the cabin farthest from the lake and closest to the parking lot."

"We'll be up by the lodge," Jamie said to Declan. "If you could bring Emma to us."

Aaron called Gage and let him know they were bringing Kelli to speak with him. "Scott is in his office, with Ryker watching over him," he told the others after the call ended. "Gage is going to meet us outside the lodge."

Gage was waiting outside when they arrived, the overhead security light casting ghastly shadows over his features.

"Sergeant Walker, this is Kelli," Jamie introduced the girl. "She needs to report a crime."

"Yeah. A crime." Kelli lifted her chin. "Mr. Sprague has been molesting girls at the camp. He molested me, and threatened me, and I think he did the same with Olivia. That's probably why she ran away."

Gage glanced at Aaron, who nodded. "You have a statement about all this?" he asked Jamie.

"Yes, sir. It wasn't a stranger who attacked a camper behind the pit toilet tonight. It was Mr. Sprague."

"Did you stab Mr. Sprague with a coat hanger?" Gage asked Kelli.

"Is that what happened to him?" Kelli shook her head. "I didn't do it, but I wish I had."

"I think Willa stabbed Scott," Aaron said. "She heard Kelli cry out and went to investigate. She shouted at Scott to stop and that startled him enough that Kelli was able to get away. But now Willa is missing. Declan found her phone behind the pit toilet." He held up the evidence bag with the phone inside.

"Where is Scott now?" Jake asked.

"He's in his office," Gage said. "Ryker is keeping him there. His story about rescuing a camper who was being attacked by a mysterious stranger didn't add up to me."

"Don't believe anything he says," Kelli said. "He lies all the time."

Gage's radio crackled and he answered the summons. "Sergeant, I've over here at Willow Cabin. Emma Agnew is fine. No sign of Scott."

Gage sent a questioning look to Jamie, but Kelli answered him. "Emma is my little sister. Mr. Sprague threatened her if I didn't do what he wanted. I asked the deputy to make sure she was okay."

"You say you think Mr. Sprague was molesting Olivia Pryor?" Gage asked.

"I don't have any proof," Kelli said. "But he didn't start bothering me until she was gone. And why else would she run away? If it hadn't been for Emma, I might have tried to leave, too."

"We need to contact your parents," Gage said. "Where do they live?"

"Pennsylvania," Kelli said.

Gage checked his watch. "It's after midnight there."

"I can contact them, sir," Jamie said. "Kelli can speak with them. I'm sure they'll want to come down as soon as possible."

"What do I do until they get here?" Kelli asked. "I don't want to stay here at camp."

"We'll speak with your parents," Jamie said. "But if it's all right with them, you and Emma can stay with me and my husband. He's a law enforcement officer, too. My sister and our infant daughter live with us. You'll be safe there."

Kelli smiled. "It will be like having two bodyguards."

"Speak with the Agnews," Gage said. "I'll see to Sprague."

"There's a side parlor we can use to make the call, over there." Kelli pointed to a doorway to their left.

When Jamie and Kelli had left, Aaron turned to Gage. "I want to talk to Scott," he said.

"What about?" Gage asked.

"I want to ask him about Willa. What happened when she interrupted him and Kelli?"

"He may not tell you anything."

"I still want to ask."

Gage nodded. "Come with me."

Ryker stepped aside to let them into the office. Scott was seated behind his desk, fresh scratches on his face glowing red in the bright overhead light that bleached the rest of his skin the color of a puffball mushroom.

"I've telephoned my lawyer and I don't have to say anything else to you," he said.

"All I want to know is where is Willa?" Aaron asked.

Scott frowned. "Who is Willa? We don't have a camper by that name."

"She's not a camper," Aaron said. "She's a nurse. Her phone was found behind that pit toilet. Where you were fighting with your alleged assailant."

"There is no 'alleged' assailant. I was attacked."

"How's the leg?" Gage asked. "I'll bet it hurts."

"No thanks to you."

"You could have gone to the hospital with the paramedics," Gage said.

"I don't need a hospital."

"I don't know." Gage peered over the desk at Scott's leg. "Those marshmallow roasting sticks probably aren't the most sanitary things."

Sprague glared at him, then rose. "I'm going to bed."

"First, would you like to tell us about Kelli?"

"I don't know any Kelli."

"She's a camper here," Gage said. "Long brown hair. Twelve years old. She says you were molesting her behind the pit toilet when Willa Reynolds interrupted you. She ran away. You struggled with Willa and she stabbed you with a coat hanger used to roast marshmallows."

Scott's expression remained impassive. "I don't know what you're talking about. And that's all I'm saying until I see my lawyer."

"Fine." Gage turned to Ryker. "You and Shane take him to the station and book him."

"Book me for what?" Scott roared. "I've done nothing wrong."

"Mr. Sprague, you're being charged with sexual assault of a child by one in a position of trust, for a start. There may be other charges forthcoming. You have the right to remain silent…" Gage recited the full Miranda warning while Scott gaped at him.

Ryker moved forward and cuffed Scott's hands behind his back. Scott remained silent, though he glared at them all, eyes dark with rage.

Chapter Eighteen

While other deputies took Scott Sprague to jail, Aaron, Jake and Declan stayed behind at the camp to search for Willa. Aaron started by calling Gary. As he listened to the phone ring, he paced, hoping to hear that Willa had found her own way home and was sleeping peacefully. She might be upset with Aaron for deserting her, but she would be safe.

"Hello?" Gary answered. He sounded groggy.

"Gary, this is Aaron. Is Willa there?"

"Why are you asking me? Why not call her? And aren't you supposed to be with her?"

"There was a problem here at the camp and we got separated. She must have dropped her phone, because we found it, but I can't find her. I was hoping she got a ride home with someone else."

"Let me check her room."

Shuffling noises, then a long silence. Aaron began to wonder if the call had disconnected when Gary's voice came back on the line. He sounded wide-awake now. "She's not here. Her bed hasn't been slept in. What's going on? What kind of problem at the camp? Where are you now?"

"I'm still at the camp. Have you heard from Willa at all tonight?"

"No. Not since she left to meet up with you. She said you

were going to the bonfire at the camp to snoop around for more evidence about what might have happened to Olivia. Why isn't Willa with you?"

Aaron blew out a breath. He didn't want to upset Gary, but clearly the man was already upset. "Scott was caught with a camper, one of the older girls, behind one of the pit toilets tonight," he said. "Willa interrupted them. The camper got away and Scott has been arrested, but we can't find Willa."

"Wait—Scott was with a camper. Like—how was he with her?"

"We believe he was molesting her."

"Oh, wow."

"Were there ever rumors about that kind of thing among the staff?"

"No." Aaron pictured Gary shaking his head. "I never heard anything like that. You're saying Willa interrupted them—what happened?"

"We're not sure, except that the camper got away and Willa dropped her phone. There may have been a struggle, but we're not sure."

"What does Scott say?"

"He's not talking."

Gary swore under his breath. "Let me come down there. I can help look for her."

"No. I need you to stay there in case Willa shows up or tries to contact you."

A long silence. Finally Gary said, "All right. But you promise to call me as soon as you know anything."

"I promise." He ended the call and turned to the others. "Her brother hasn't heard from her. Let's go."

But finding their way in the darkness, especially after clouds moved in to cover the moon, proved more difficult than Aaron had imagined. They could detect no indication of which way Willa had gone. After Declan fell on the rocks and Jake got tangled in a stretch of barbed wire fence, they halted.

"We need to wait until daylight," Jake said. "We can get Anna Trent and her search dog, Jacqui, out here, plus we can call in search and rescue to assist. All we're doing now is risking ourselves and possibly obscuring the trail more."

Aaron kicked at the dirt, frustrated. "You're right," he said.

Jake clapped him on the back. "Remember—we caught Scott minutes after Willa surprised him with Kelli. He didn't have time to spirit her away. And there was no blood at the scene but Scott's own, so it's unlikely he hurt her badly."

"Then where is she?" Aaron asked.

"We're going to find her," Jake said. "Tomorrow."

Aaron let them persuade him to get in his truck and leave, but as soon as they were out of sight, he turned around and went back to the camp parking lot. If this was as close as he could be to Willa right now, then this was where he would stay. He pulled a sleeping bag out from the back of the vehicle and spread it on the front seat and crawled in.

He didn't sleep. He didn't even try. Instead, he sat and stared out the windshield, going over the events of the last few hours. How had they missed that Scott was responsible? They could have at least asked the campers if any of the staff had behaved inappropriately toward them. True, there had been no evidence pointing them in that direction, but if they had dug deeper, would they have found some? Was he a bad cop because he hadn't figured this out?

He had so many questions, none of them with answers.

But the one that hurt the most kept repeating in his mind: Would Willa forgive him for failing her again?

WILLA WOKE, stiff from sleeping on the floor of the rock shelter, and checked her watch: 6:30 a.m. She sat up, and Olivia stirred beside her.

"What time is it?" the girl asked.

Willa told her and Olivia groaned and pulled the blanket over her head. "I want to get back to camp before everyone wakes up," Willa said. "We can call the sheriff's department before Scott knows what's going on."

Olivia pushed off the blanket. "You're right." She sat up. "I can heat water for tea, but there's nothing for breakfast."

"I'd rather wait until we get to camp." Olivia's herb tea was a poor substitute for real coffee.

Olivia yawned. "Then I'll pack up and we'll get started."

Five minutes later, the girl had the blanket, sleeping bag and little stove shoved into or strapped to her pack. She led the way out of the shelter, pushing the pack in front of her.

Pink streaked the sky as they set off through the woods. Willa pulled her sweater around her in the early-morning chill. Olivia didn't seem to notice, though she slowed her own brisk pace when she noticed Willa limping.

"I forgot about your ankle," Olivia said. "Does it hurt much?"

"Not that much," Willa lied. "I'll be fine once we get to camp." Though she had spoken confidently about the unlikelihood of running into Scott Sprague at this early hour, her memory of the story Olivia had told her about Scott's violence toward Trevor Lawson sent tendrils of fear through her.

"It's not much farther," Olivia said. "I lucked out, finding that hiding place so close to camp. It made it easier to slip over here to steal food and supplies, and keep an eye on Mr. Sprague. And I figured no one would expect me to be so nearby."

A few moments later, they reached a barbed wire fence. Oliva halted and waited for Willa to catch up with her.

"When we cross this, we'll be on Mountain Kingdom property," Olivia said. "Where should we go? Not the office. I don't want to risk seeing Mr. Sprague."

Willa took her hand. "I'm not going to let him hurt you." Though realistically, she knew she couldn't stop him by herself. "We'll avoid Scott, though, and find someone else to help us." Someone who would contact the sheriff's department.

"I'm really nervous about going back," Olivia said. "Mr. Sprague is really evil, and he knows a lot of important people."

"The sheriff and his deputies don't care how important someone is if they've done something wrong." Aaron believed that, and he had said the sheriff was a good man. She took the girl's hand. "And I'm not going to leave you. Not until I'm sure you're safe."

Olivia squeezed her hand. "Thanks." She faced forward again, and took a deep breath. "I'm ready now. Let's do this."

Olivia slipped through the strands of wire, and waited for Willa to follow.

They set out at a faster pace now. "This is my favorite time to come here," Olivia said. "No one is around. You could walk away with half the camp and no one would know."

They made a wide berth around Scott's cabin, then passed the remains of the bonfire, the smell of woodsmoke still hanging in the air. Olivia detoured to grab a partial bag of marshmallows someone had left on a bench in the boat house. She offered the bag to Willa, who declined, but Olivia stuffed two in her mouth.

"Why don't you have a phone?" Olivia asked after she had swallowed the marshmallows. "I just now thought of that. I'm so used to no one around here having a phone, since we all have to give them up when we get here. But you could have called for help."

"I lost it, either when I was struggling with Scott, or when I ran away."

"How did you get away from him?"

"I stabbed him in the thigh with a bent coat hanger I'd been using to roast marshmallows."

Olivia clapped her hand over her mouth to stifle a laugh. "Oh, that's perfect. The only thing better would be if it was still hot—and if you could have aimed a little more toward the center."

Willa smiled, and looked toward the parking lot, then stopped.

"What is it?" Olivia moved in close beside her. "Did you see someone? Is it Sprague?"

"I see someone, but it's not Scott." She took Olivia's hand. "Come on. This is one of the good guys."

Aaron had just climbed out of his truck when he saw them walking toward him. He didn't run, just waited, but when they were close enough, he moved forward and enveloped them both in a hug. Then he stepped back and looked at the girl.

"You must be Olivia."

She nodded.

"I'm Aaron," he said. "Deputy Aaron Ames. We arrested Scott Sprague last night."

Olivia began to sob. Aaron and Willa moved in to hold her, letting her cry until she had no more tears left.

When the girl had quieted, Aaron looked at Willa. "You're hurt." He started to touch the side of her face, then drew back.

Willa hadn't seen her face, but she could feel the swelling of her lip and around her eye. "Scott hit me pretty good. But it will heal."

"She sprained her ankle, too," Olivia said. "But not before she stabbed Mr. Sprague with a marshmallow roaster."

"That was one of the things that made us suspicious of his story that he had chased off a stranger who was attacking a camper," Aaron said.

"I'm glad you didn't believe him," Olivia said.

"Are you sure you're okay?" Aaron asked Willa. "Do I need to call someone?"

"It's not too bad, really," Willa said. At the moment, the joint was throbbing, but she didn't care. That, too, would heal. "You don't need to call anyone. We just need to get away from here."

"Then let's go." They got into Aaron's truck, Olivia in the back seat, and he headed away from the camp.

Aaron called the sheriff directly. Travis was awake, though he wasn't at the sheriff's department yet.

"What have you got?" the sheriff asked when he answered the phone.

"I have Olivia with me," Aaron said. "And Willa."

The sheriff's relieved sigh was audible down the line. "Are they all right?"

"Willa has a sprained ankle and a few bruises. They're fine otherwise." He gave Olivia a questioning look.

"I'm hungry," Olivia said. Then more softly she added, "And I'd really like to see my parents."

"I'll call your parents," Travis said. "Meet us at the sheriff's department."

Aaron started to protest that Willa needed to see a doctor, but she laid her hand on his.

"Let's take Olivia to her parents," she said. "I'll be fine." She smiled. "And I'm hungry, too."

Mr. and Mrs. Pryor were waiting in the sheriff's office when Aaron, Willa and Olivia arrived. Sylvia Pryor burst into tears and Olivia started crying, too. The others looked on at the touching reunion.

Aaron moved closer to the sheriff. "Where is Scott?" he whispered.

"He's in the jail in Junction," Travis said. "I'm going down there later today to question him, after his lawyer gets here from Denver."

"Do you think he'll tell you anything?"

"Probably not, but we don't need his statement. Between what Kelli has told us and what Olivia will tell us, we shouldn't have any problem proving the charges."

The Pryors finally released their hold on the girl. "I know you're all anxious to be done with this ordeal," Travis said. "But we're going to need a statement from Olivia." He glanced at Willa. "And from you, too."

"Can I at least have breakfast first?" Olivia asked, a plaintive whine edging her words.

"It's on the way," he said.

Aaron wondered what restaurant had agreed to cater breakfast at this hour, but voices rose and the door opened to admit an attractive brunette, followed by office manager Adelaide Kinkaid and two toddlers.

"I hope you like waffles," the younger woman called as she passed.

They followed the women and children into the conference room at the end of the hall, where they began unloading a bin full of food dishes—waffles, scrambled eggs, sausages, hash browns and biscuits.

"This is my wife, Lacey," Travis introduced the younger woman. "And our office manager, Adelaide Kinkaid."

"And this is Casey and Kelsey." Lacey put a hand on the top of each toddler's head. The two children grinned up at them.

"I love waffles," Olivia said. She eyed the spread hungrily. "Thank you."

Aaron realized that he, too, was suddenly ravenous. They all filled their plates, then ate without saying much for the next fifteen or twenty minutes.

Finally, Olivia pushed away her plate. "That was so much better than leftovers and granola bars," she said.

"Is that what you've been eating?" her mother asked.

"It wasn't so bad," Olivia said.

"I don't understand any of this," her mother said. "Would someone please tell us what happened?"

"I'll let Olivia do that," Travis said. "When she's ready."

"I'm ready," Olivia said. "I want to tell you everything."

"Then come with me." Travis stood. Olivia and her parents followed him down the hall to an interview room. "Wait until we're done here," he instructed Willa and Aaron.

They sat alone in the conference room, amid the remains of breakfast. For a long time, neither said anything, too weary or stunned or overwhelmed to speak.

Finally, Aaron turned to her. "I don't have words to describe how glad I was to see you this morning," he said. "I spent the night telling myself you were probably all right, but it's hard not to think of the worst." He stilled as a thought struck him. "You should call Gary. He's probably worried sick."

"I don't have my phone," she said.

"We'll have to get that for you later." He handed her his phone and she called her brother and reassured him she was all right.

"I'll tell you all about it later," she said. "Right now I'm waiting to give a statement to the sheriff." She glanced at Aaron. "Yes, he's with me. I'm using his phone... I will, I promise."

She ended the call and returned his phone. "Gary says hello. A friend from camp already called to tell him Scott was arrested. I told him I'd fill him in on more details later."

"I want to hear everything, too," Aaron said. "But I won't ask you to go through it twice."

"What happened with Scott?" she asked. "How did he end up in custody?"

"The girl he was with when you interrupted his attack on her told us how he had targeted and threatened her. And she told us about you making it possible for her to escape Scott's clutches. She didn't know who you were or what happened after she ran away, but after we found your phone behind the pit toilets we put two and two together. I wanted to believe you had run away and were safe, but we just didn't know. We tried to search for you in the dark, but it's impossible in that rough country." He frowned. "Where were you all night?"

"I was with Olivia. She had a pretty comfortable hide-out fixed up in a space between two boulders. She's a re-markable girl."

He glanced down. "How's your ankle?"

"It hurts." She reached down and slipped off her shoe. "I'm sure it's just a sprain, but I should wrap it and keep it elevated."

"Let me see." He beckoned and after a moment's hesitation, she lifted her foot into his lap. He began massaging very gently, his hands warm and soothing. She closed her eyes and sighed. He watched the tension leave her face and his throat tightened as he thought of how close he had come to losing her.

Behind them, someone cleared their throat. Willa opened her eyes and pulled her foot from his lap as he turned to see Adelaide frowning at them. "The sheriff is ready for you now."

Aaron stood. "Thanks, Adelaide. And thanks for the breakfast."

"Yes, thank you," Willa said as she and Aaron slid past her into the hallway.

"OLIVIA'S PARENTS ARE taking her to the hospital to have her examined," Travis said when they joined him in the interview room. "She's a strong little girl." Though he had dark circles beneath his eyes, the sheriff looked energized. They all probably felt that way. After so many days and nights of searching, Olivia had been found safe, and they had a man who had hurt a lot of people behind bars.

"Olivia is amazing," Willa agreed. "I was stumbling around in the dark, lost, and she found me and took me to her hideout, gave me tea, offered to share her food and promised to lead me back to the camp in the morning. While we've all been worried sick about her alone in the wilderness, she was doing a pretty good job of taking care of herself, though she admitted the novelty of the situation was wearing off and she'd be glad to get back to her parents."

"Did she tell you her story?" Travis asked.

"Yes. Does it fit with what you know about Trevor Lawson's death?"

"It does."

"What about Trevor Lawson?" Aaron asked.

"Why don't you tell us what you know." Travis nodded to Willa.

She spread her hands flat on the table in front of her. How to tell everything she had learned in the past twelve hours, without talking for half a day?

"The night before she disappeared, Olivia says Trevor caught Scott molesting her and they fought," she began. "Scott tied up Lawson, made him drink a bottle of whiskey and forced pills down his throat, then walked him to the parking lot. Olivia didn't see anything after that. It sounds like Trevor got into his car, tried to drive home and in his intoxicated state was unable to keep the car on the road."

"Or Scott followed him and made sure he ran off the road," Aaron said.

"That last may be difficult to prove, but we'll investigate it," Travis said. "Maybe someone spotted Scott's car on the road behind Lawson." He turned to Willa once more. "Now let's hear what happened to you."

She told her story, from the moment she spotted Kelli waiting for someone by the bonfire until she and Olivia reunited with Aaron that morning. "After hearing Olivia's and Kelli's stories, I wonder how many other children that man has harmed," she said.

"We'll put out a plea for other current and former campers who may have information to come forward," Travis said. "That may result in more charges." He stood. "Go home, both of you. Get some rest. We'll be in touch if we have further questions."

Aaron rose. "I start night shift this evening," he said. "I'll be in then."

She and Aaron left together "Do you think Olivia is

going to be all right?" he asked when they were in his truck, headed back to Eagle Mountain.

"I think so. She's been through a lot, but she's a very resilient girl. And she'll have her parents. They'll get her the help she needs." She shifted toward him. "What about Scott? What's going to happen to him?"

"Some of it depends on how many other girls he molested, and who will testify against him. And on what charges he faces in relation to Trevor's death."

Gary met them at the front door and pulled Willa into a tight hug. When he stepped back, her eyes were shiny with unshed tears. "Did Scott do that to your face?" Gary asked.

She nodded. Gary made a growling sound. "I made coffee," he said. "Come and tell me what happened."

They followed him into the kitchen and sat around the table, and the two men listened as Willa retold Olivia's story of witnessing the torture of Trevor Lawson, and about Sprague's habit of abusing girls.

"Just as well I didn't know that about him," Gary said. "I'd have been tempted to ruin some tools on him."

"With the evidence of the two girls and what we know about Trevor's death, I think Scott will be locked up for a very long time," Aaron said.

Gary wrapped both hands around his coffee mug and studied them both. "Are you two friends again?" he asked.

Aaron looked at Willa, awaiting her answer. She took his hand in hers. "I never stopped loving you," she said.

"Ha! I knew it," Gary said.

Aaron looked at him. "What I can't understand is why you don't hate me," he said. "You almost went to trial for a murder you didn't commit. Even so, your life was pretty much ruined because of the accusations against you."

"I didn't go to trial." He drained his coffee mug and set

it down with a thump. "The DA knew a bad case when he saw one. And my life wasn't ruined. I like it here in Eagle Mountain. The only thing I hated was how miserable Willa was. She was upset about what happened to me and all the harassment, but what she really missed was you."

"I never stopped loving you," he told her. "And I'll never stop apologizing for what I did to tear us apart."

She raised their clasped hands and kissed the back of his. "I'm as much to blame as you are," she said. "So let's forgive each other. We both came to Eagle Mountain to make a fresh start, so let's do that."

"Together."

"Yes, together."

Gary stood. "I'm outta here. Have fun kissing and making up."

He left, and Aaron pulled her to him. "I like the way your brother thinks," he said, and kissed her.

She took his hand and pulled him toward her bedroom. "We have a lot of catching up to do," she said.

Aaron followed willingly. They would never get back the months they had lost, but they had years to build a love that would last.

Epilogue

New Evidence Leads to Killer

Waterbury police announced today that they have charged Albert Wayne Terriot with the murder of Rachel Sherman two years ago. Rachel was abducted from Deer Hollow Youth Camp and her body was later found in a nearby creek. She had been strangled. Though police had identified several persons of interest in their initial investigation of the murder, they were never able to find proof of the real killer. A review of the case by the department's newly formed Cold Case Squad this year led to the discovery of previously untested items found at the crime scene. This led to the construction of a DNA profile that was eventually linked to Terriot. The now-fifty-eight-year-old Terriot was never on law enforcement's radar as a suspect before this new DNA evidence linked him to the crime.

Police Detective Darrel Green said law enforcement now believe Terriot was the mysterious vagrant living in the woods near the camp that several campers told stories about at the time. Law enforcement was unable to find any proof of the vagrant's existence at that time and dismissed the story as something children invented to scare each other.

Terriot was convicted of an attack on another minor child in Chester, Vermont, last year and is currently serving a fifteen-year sentence for that crime. Washington County District Attorney Randall Freed says he expects Terriot to be tried for Rachel's murder some time next year.

"Do you feel like a big weight is off your shoulders?" Willa asked Gary when she met him for lunch the day after Aaron sent her a link to the story about Albert Terriot's arrest.

"Yeah," Gary said. He traced a line of condensation down his water glass with one thumb. "I told myself I was past all that, but knowing they'll never come back and try to pin the crime on me is a big relief."

"For me, too," she admitted. "I always worried about you."

"I'm good. What about you? Things going okay with Aaron?"

"They are. We're good together." She glanced down, unable to stop admiring the sapphire solitaire he had recently given her, two months to the day after she had moved in with him.

"So when's the wedding?" Gary asked.

"We're waiting to schedule it until after Bethany's wedding. We don't want to take any attention away from her. What about you? You're not too lonely in the house without me there?"

"I like my privacy. Always have. And it's easier to sleep during the day without someone else there."

She made a face. "How long will you be on night shift?"

"Don't know. Until they hire someone with less experience than me. But I like it. Emergency dispatch isn't as busy at night around here, so it's a good way to ease into the job."

"But you still like the work?" She tried to keep the concern out of her voice. Gary didn't like it when he suspected her of babying him.

"Yeah, I do. It's not something I ever thought I'd be doing, but it's really interesting. And I'm helping people, which is good, too." He pointed a french fry at her. "I'm pretty sure I only got the position because Aaron recommended me. But he won't admit it."

"He still feels guilty about accusing you of murder."

"That's in the past now. It all worked out. And I'm happy you're happy."

"I am." Happier than she would have thought possible. "He's a good man," she said.

"He is. And he's lucky to have you."

"What about you?" she asked. "Are you seeing anyone? There's a new nurse at the clinic…"

He shook his head. "Don't go there," he said. "I'll find my own dates, thank you very much."

"All right. All right." She would never stop wanting to look after her little brother, but she was willing to relax, for now. Gary seemed to be doing well, and she wanted to focus on her own life, and the future. With Aaron, and, if things worked out, their children.

"You've gone all dreamy-eyed again," Gary said. He laughed. "It's good to see it."

She only smiled and nodded. Life was good, and she wasn't going to take that for granted for a single moment.

* * * * *

*If you missed the first book in Cindi Myers's
Eagle Mountain: Unsolved Mysteries miniseries,
look for* Canyon Killer, *available now.
And keep an eye out for upcoming titles in the series,
coming soon, only from Harlequin Intrigue!*